Ginger & Klaus
A Hitch in the Harvest
By Kory Labarga

TABLE OF CONTENTS

CHAPTER 1
The Most Festive Cookie in the World

Ginger leaned against the interior of the concrete pipe that ran under Sprinkleton, watching as the Mice of Sweetfort (formerly the Colony Behind the Cabinets) busied themselves with a variety of important tasks. Ever since King Shol's defeat at the hands of the Voles of Cowtown on Independence Day—concluding with the death of Shol himself—there had been a steady influx of leaderless rodents seeking refuge in the storm drain, and now the colony's numbers had more than quadrupled. *That's for the best*, she mused, watching as a mouse half her size, recently newborn and still pink and furless, attempted to erect a wooden stake. *The voles want Sprinkleton all to themselves, but as long as King Klaus and the growing resistance have something to say about it, they don't stand a chance.*

Yes, it was *King Klaus* now, although her murine friend had accepted the title with no small amount of hesitation. His coronation had gone off without a hitch (mostly), and ever since then, the humble regent had instituted laws and sanctioned defensive projects that had improved the community and promised a better future. Within the storm drain, the Colony had built a number of homes—cardboard patched together with bits of string— built upon rafters that were high enough to withstand the occasional downpour outside; the construction had finally ended just a couple of weeks ago, and now the mice were building walls of cardboard, watchtowers of tin boxes and sticks on the eastern and western sides of the village, and cheval-de-frise comprised of intersecting rose stems. Ginger much preferred the quaint space behind the cabinets where she had first met Klaus, but she understood that it was far too small for such a crowd, and history had shown that it could be easily breached.

The Cookies of Theo did not live with the mice there at "Sweetfort," as Klaus affectionately called it, but for the preservation of the Fur-Crumb Alliance, visits were frequent. Ginger, Molasses, Agapa, Reinhard, Dave, and the other remaining cookies of Mount Oniz helped where they could— if not with construction, then with morale, or with reconnaissance missions designed to obtain updates on the Voles of Cowtown or the Cookies of Tanas. While rumors were swirling about the voles setting their sights upon Sprinkleton and the surrounding fields, the Alliance had not heard a peep about Tanas or his minions. The traitor, Frostina, as well as those who had followed in her rebellion, had vanished; equally alarming was that Clove, her torturer, and Limerence, who had struck her with an arrow on Valentine's Eve, were missing. For all she knew, they could be in another country by now—possibly Sweden, or maybe even Russia!

She looked down at the end of her left arm and frowned. The wound that Clove had delivered to her was still there; Mr. Theo had not summoned her to his kitchen to mend her, nor had the lamb cookie—who had caused the quake and storm on Independence Day, she was quite sure— checked in with her and offered his aid. In fact, she had not seen hide nor hair nor crumb of the lamb ever since she had watched him bound off the roof of a shack nearly five months ago. Where had everyone gone? What were they so busy doing? Didn't they love her company? Who *wouldn't*?

Klaus was a little too busy enjoying the company of someone *else* to spend much time with her, and she knew she had no right to throw a tantrum over it; Klaus *was* a married mouse now, after all, and his primary duty was to his bride, Ingrid. Their nuptials had taken place the same day as his coronation, back in September. It had been a lovely event, one that had moved many in attendance to tears, and that had given her a most earnest desire for tear ducts. The Mice of Sweetfort had thoughtfully constructed Klaus's house first, granting the newlyweds their very own spacious place to begin their marriage. As expected, Klaus had protested both the special treatment and the size of his new home, but his friends—directed by Horace—had ignored every word. The couple was there now, preparing for the festivities that they had planned for the evening.

Finally, some quality time with my best friend, she thought. Ginger, Molasses, and select others would be granted an audience with the busy king. Today was a day that the humans called *Thanksgiving*, and that the mice called *Harvest*—a day of gratitude, fellowship, and overeating. Ginger had found it a kind gesture for the mice to invite the cookies to their Harvest dinner, even though cookies did not possess tastebuds, esophagi, intestines, or anything else that would permit them to enjoy food in any way. It was the thought that counted...assuming that the mice were not thinking that the cookies would serve as fine desserts after supper.

Ginger had to admit that she had come to Sweetfort too early in the day (an unfortunate byproduct of her fascination with holidays and desire to spend time with her friends), but it was not for *completely* selfish reasons; she had heard that Harvest was one of the biggest events of the year for the mice of the vale, and she wished to help out in any way she could. Indeed, even Molasses, Agapa, Reinhard, and Dave were there with her, and they had not, by any means, joined her under compulsion. No, their presence was *totally* voluntary, despite her incessant pleading over the past week that they tag along first thing Harvest morning. She tried to ignore the occasional yawn and the "staring into the void" that she observed in Molasses and Reinhard, who were usually still tucked into their gingerbeds at this time. It made no sense to her. Why would a cookie need to sleep in, anyway?

The rest of her merry band formed a semicircle outside Klaus's house. It was quite the impressive structure, she thought, and not for the first time. Stairs, comprised of horizontally stacked dominoes, led the way to a porch—which itself was an empty sunglasses case in the shape of a rectangular prism standing on a brick rafter. Atop the case, on the right and left, were two plastic cylinders—candy containers, judging by their wrappers—that stood as pillars, which lifted a cardboard patio directly above the porch. The house proper was a small crate stacked atop a larger crate—both made of real wood—with a front door and a door leading to the upstairs from the porch. Hanging on the front door was a wreath fashioned of intertwined wheat, acorn cupules, and tiny yellow flowers. Christmas lights had been stapled to every edge of the crate, casting red, green, gold, and white light almost a meter out and giving any newcomer the impression that Christmas was perpetually celebrated in Sweetfort.

Just as Reinhard was beginning to grow antsy (the antlered chap could never stand still for long), the front door swung open, and out stepped a lithe, well-groomed, brown mouse. He descended the steps and greeted the group with a bow so low that his whiskers grazed the dusty concrete. When he returned to a standing position, he placed both paws against his sides and said, "Welcome, oh bakéd ones, to the Kingly House of Klaus the Mouse! The bellhop has informed me that you seek an audience with his Highness earlier than that which was originally scheduled. I must offer my sincerest apologies, for the King and the missus are quite inundated with tasks in preparation for tonight's supper—you understand."

Ginger narrowed her frosting eyes. "There's no way that Klaus is onboard with this pretentiousness and this, this—Brother, what's that word for 'using too much flowery language'?"

"Magniloquence," said Molasses, his eyes narrowing even more than his sister's.

"Yeah, that." She raised one arm toward the butler. "I was locked away for five months in Shol's Funland with that mouse. King or no, he's my friend, and I want to see him."

The rodent wrinkled his nose and pulled out a shred of paper, which looked to have been torn from a lined notebook. With his other paw, he fished a tiny piece of graphite from his pocket. "I see," he told her. "And what is the purpose of your visit?"

"We want to help get everything ready for tonight," said Ginger. "Klaus is opening his house to guests; the least we could do is take some responsibilities off his plate. Ruling a kingdom carries enough stress. He doesn't need to worry about hanging a bunch of banners or sweeping the floor."

The mouse pressed one end of the graphite to his cheek. "The King said that he was not to be disturbed while he went about his preparations. No exceptions."

"Eh, Chester, let the poor cookies in," demanded a voice coming from behind Ginger. She turned to see Horace approaching, hobbling along on his cherry-stem cane. Although she had seen him just two months earlier, officiating the wedding of Klaus and Ingrid, he seemed to have aged significantly, the fur on his snout and upper half of his body gray and tousled. The limp in his step was more pronounced and the hunch in his back more noticeable as he leaned heavily on his cane. "These cookies are as kin to our dear king, and he would be most...*unjoyed* to learn you had turned 'em away."

Chester's eyes grew as large as boulders. "Is this— Ginger? *The* Ginger?" He offered a quick bow as an apology. "I—I did not know. I am quite new here! Third day, as a matter of fact."

"Don' make it any worse, boy," said Horace with a smirk. He placed a paw where Ginger's shoulder might have been and proceeded to lead her and her friends up the steps. "The Cookies of Theo are always welcome in the House of Klaus or anywhere else in Sweetfort. Klaus will be delighted to see you, even if you *are* twelve hours early."

"Horace, dear sir," said Agapa, her wings fluttering as she followed the group abreast of Dave. Her bow, conspicuously absent from her hands, rested on her back. "A question, if I may?"

"O' course, miss."

"I am altogether unfamiliar with the holiday that you mice call 'Harvest.' Would you care to explain? I would prefer not to be 'out of the loop,' as the expression goes, as we fellowship this eve."

Horace cast a glance back at her. "'Tis is the season of harvest, muh dear. The humans sow crops in the spring and summer that be ripe for pickin' in October and November, an' more often than not, they've more produce than they actually need. That's where we come in, see. We reap the benefits o' what the Sprinkletonians've sown, eating a—a *array* of these goods all at once on Harvest night. 'Tis a time to sit wi' one's friends and family an' to reflect on the mult'udinous provisions that've come into our lives over the weeks, months, or years. Thinkin' on these things, we express our gratitude out loud fer all to hear."

"That sounds like a holiday we cookies should celebrate, too," Reinhard noted. "After all, has not Mr. Theo himself commanded us to be thankful in all circumstances?"

"He has," replied Agapa, "and I am all the more gladdened by the invitation extended by Klaus. Thank you for the explanation, Mister Horace."

The mouse smiled and pressed open the front door. Ginger had been inside Klaus's house before, but its warmth and coziness never failed to amaze her. White Christmas lights outlined the inner edges of the crate, brightening the room and filling it with welcoming color, but not at the risk of blinding its inhabitants. The top left-hand corner of the room was a kitchen carpeted by a circular white doily; blocks of cheese covered half the surface area of the fabric, and a pile of vegetable chunks, nuts, and seeds took up the other half. Three crayon boxes stood on their sides at the edge of this makeshift kitchen and formed an L-shape, their smooth surfaces used as a counter. The bottom left-hand section of the room resembled a library, with the lids of pill bottles for chairs and inscribed leaflets—each the size of a human's thumb—stacked against the walls. The bottom right-hand corner, to Ginger's right, was the "war room," fitted with an assortment of weapons and armor on display, a central cardboard-box table with a map unfurled across its surface, and diagrams of battle strategies on every centimeter of wall. The top right-hand corner of the room was the dining area, with a lengthy nightstand leg for a table and the lids of ten ring boxes serving as cushioned seats. Between the kitchen and the dining area, and placed against the two walls at the back of the room just as they turned into the staircase leading to the second floor, were the thrones for the two rulers—the throne on the right for Klaus and the throne on the left for Ingrid. Stairs, made of additional stacked dominoes, could be ascended to reach the bedrooms upstairs; Klaus had allowed Ginger to room in one of the two guest quarters about a month ago, and it was there that she had experienced the best sleep of her short life.

Klaus was, as Ginger had expected, pacing across the room with a frantic look on his face, tucking away clutter, and dusting shelves and surfaces. Ingrid was busy balancing on one of the ring box lids and attempting to pin a banner that read "Happy Harvest" to the ceiling. The house was cozy, but it was also a *mess*; it appeared that Klaus must have had company over the previous night, for half-empty plates rested on the table beside forgotten documents, leftover food mottled the kitchen counter, and leaflets were scattered across the library rather than consolidated with the stacks that were piled against the wall. If Ginger were a more selfish cookie, she would have tiptoed (a figure of speech, since she had not a single toe to speak of) out of the house and returned in the evening to a more organized house. She never *could* stand an untidy living space, as Molasses—who was ever pestered by her over-the-top rules in their gingerbread house—could attest.

Klaus was so caught up in his manic scouring that he failed to notice his guests for half a minute, and Horace had to tap his back to get him to turn around. Once he saw Ginger, he nearly dropped a wedge of cheese—not because he was excited to see her, Ginger understood, but because he was surprised that she and her friends had arrived well ahead of schedule.

"Happy Harvest, Klaus and Ingrid!" she exclaimed, throwing both arms as wide as she could. "Surprise! We're early! And we're here to take some chores off your paws."

"She insisted on helping, the kind lass," said Horace.

Klaus managed to shake aside his astonishment and ran across the room to embrace her. "Happy Harvest, my dear Ginger! You're most welcome here—all of you! You never need an invitation. And your help is most welcome, as well."

"More than you know," Ingrid said with a chuckle. "I think my husband was ready to pull his fur out. A bald king—can you imagine?"

Ginger went to Ingrid and gave her a hug, and the other cookies exchanged pleasantries with their hosts. Then Klaus sat on his throne with a weary huff and leaned forward, clasping one paw in the other. The image brought a grin to Ginger's face. Eleven months ago, she had met this mouse in a throne room behind a cabinet; he had been wearing the same brown and blue leather clothes that he wore now, as well as the same black boots. This throne was a replica of the original, a grand chair of cardboard and matches stitched together—and Ingrid's throne mirrored it. Ginger marveled at how much had changed in nearly a year. Last December, Klaus had been called "King" by only fifteen mice, and now he wore a gold crown, and many rodents across the vale had pledged their allegiance to him. What was more, the Cookies of Theo had agreed to make him head of the Alliance, with Ginger and Molasses as co-heads. With all the positive changes that had taken place over the past eleven months, there was much to be thankful for.

Klaus, seeming more rested after a minute on his throne, gesticulated with his paws. "How do things go on Mount Oniz, my friends?"

"They're going smoothly," answered Molasses. "Dave has changed professions and has taken my place as foreman over the repairs on the mountain."

"Giving you the time you need to train the other cookies for the inevitable war to come," Klaus replied. "Smart."

Reinhard scoffed. "Sure, that is great and all, but wait until you hear *this*." He began to prance in place, his obvious excitement overflowing. "Mr. Theo is gearing up for Christmas! Music streams from his kitchen, swelling with sleigh bells and horns and saxophones. Already the decorations are starting to show up, and already he sets out his containers of flour, sugar, and sprinkles. It is hard to believe it is that time already!"

"We've already heard the stir from the Sprinkletonians about Mr. Theo's Christmas cookies this year," Ingrid told them. "The entire town is abuzz, and they say this will be his 'best batch ever.' No offense to present company, of course."

Klaus interlocked his claws, almost as if he were in prayer. "Maybe Mr. Theo's distribution of the boons will go more smoothly this time, now that Tanas is out of the picture."

"Do we know that he is truly out of the picture?" inquired Agapa.

"One can only hope."

"We should still assume that he can do damage— whether he is nearby or far off," Molasses suggested. "The Alliance will need to be vigilant this holiday season."

Ginger smacked the ends of her arms together. "Oh, come on now, everyone! Why are we talking about Tanas on a day like this? This is a day to celebrate! But before we celebrate, we need to get everything celebration-ready. We're all here now, so how can we help?"

Ingrid's fur bristled with enthusiasm. "So kind of you to offer, Ginger. We need a banner hung at the entryway, the leaflets stacked with the others, an almond on every small plate and a chunk of kabocha squash on every large plate, the floor swept, the picture frames tilted back to balance, the kitchen counters cleaned, and the hallways upstairs buffed. Then we'll take a break, and I'll brief you on the other half of the things that need to get done."

Dave's eyes widened. "Is she always like this?"

"I'm the strategist of our kingdom," Klaus answered with a laugh. "She's the strategist of our home. Time has shown that she knows what she's doing."

"Very well!" said Agapa. "Let us get to it, shall we?"

They discussed how they should divide the work before splitting up in teams of two, Dave being the only one to volunteer to work alone in buffing the floors upstairs. Ginger was rather taken aback when Ingrid opted to buddy up with *her* instead of her new husband, leaving Klaus to work with Molasses and Agapa to work with Reinhard.

Ginger was loath to admit that she had been hoping to get her best friend to herself for a few minutes, at least; but Ingrid, as she had learned in recent months, was a lovely and stalwart mouse, one who complemented Klaus well and who could be a great friend in her own right. Ingrid had been among the first group of mice to perceive the evil in King Shol and to defect to Klaus, whom Shol had forced out of his kingdom. Due to her excellent organizational abilities, Klaus had entrusted her with decision-making over the everyday, menial goings-on in the Colony when they had still lived behind the cabinets. Ginger had long since forgiven the mouse for calling her a "monster" back at Christmastime—or at least she *believed* she had forgiven her. It did not occupy her thoughts every hour of the day as it once had, at least.

They were shifting picture frames on the dining room wall when Ingrid nudged Ginger and looked at her with sincere eyes. "I want to thank you for joining us today," she said. "Even if cookies can't enjoy Harvest supper, it means a lot to the Alliance that you're celebrating with us. And it means a lot to me and Klaus personally." She returned her attention to the picture frame before her. "My parents loved the holidays. We used to live in a dilapidated barn on the southern side of town; that's where I grew up. We had an entire stall all to ourselves...and every Harvest, my mother and father would decorate the stall, turning a place that had once housed pigs and their filth into a place of magic. That's one thing I love about the holidays. Suddenly the mundane gets a makeover, and there is magic in the air. I always wanted to decorate my own house in honor of my parents, who went to Great Boris's furry bosom a year and a half ago."

"I'm very sorry for your loss," Ginger replied. "You're certainly doing a beautiful job. Did Klaus also grow up with that same holiday spirit?"

Ingrid laughed. "Klaus? Not so much. His mother was not all that involved in his life, and his father was too busy raising his seven brothers and his two sisters to spend time decorating their garbage bin. Klaus *was* raised in a garbage bin, you know."

Ginger's arms flew to her face. "I had no idea—because he never told me, and I can't smell anything!"

"Oh, the stink has long since passed. It lingered for a while, though. I had to take care where I stood when I spoke to him back in the early days. It was pretty bad."

"And yet you still fell in love with him. If that isn't romantic, I don't know what is."

"Right." Ingrid beamed as she straightened a portrait from her wedding day, which had been drawn by a mouse from the original Colony with a knack for artistry. "Anyway, even though Klaus didn't grow up celebrating the holidays, he has developed a fondness for them. Maybe it was seeing the infectious happiness of the Sprinkletonians as they hung their garlands and their wreaths or as they plastered stickers on their windows. Maybe it was meeting you and seeing how giddy you were at Christmastime. Or maybe it was a combination of both."

Ginger looked back at her brother, who was debating with Klaus as to the best speed and technique to utilize when cleaning a counter. "Molasses has a hard time celebrating anything other than Christmas. He told me that gingerbread cookies seem out of place during any other holiday. I respectfully disagree."

"That's obvious by the way you're dressed today," said Ingrid with a snicker that caught her husband's attention.

"Doesn't she look great?" Klaus responded from across the room. "I have to say, I think that's your best outfit yet, Ginger."

She struck a modeling pose. "Are you that surprised? I am, after all, the most festive cookie in the world."

"Oh, we're not surprised at all," Ingrid said, still giggling.

Ginger was delighted that someone had commented on her attire. During a mission earlier that month, she, Klaus, and Molasses had happened upon a dumpster behind a grocery store and had found a virtual treasure trove of goodies. Among the items was a severely dented can filled with candies in the shape of cornucopias; she had saved these just for this occasion, and three of the candies now served as buttons for her dress. She had also scrounged up orange frosting, which she had darkened into a burnt-orange color after some first-rate chemistry work (she had added a tinge of brown frosting and mixed it all together) and had applied it in a flowy fashion to distinguish her dress from her arms and legs. She had even swapped out her bow for a new one; it was white and dotted with images of pumpkins and turkeys. Objectively, she looked fabulous. Molasses, the dull oaf, had refused to change his attire other than tying a belt with a looking glass around his waist. The looking glass had been manufactured for an action figure (another of their findings during their mission earlier the month,) but that did not stop Molasses from using it to gawk out at the horizon, at suspicious characters, or, more often than not, nothing at all.

"So when is it your turn to have all this?" Ingrid asked abruptly, motioning at their surroundings. "When will Mr. and Mrs. Ginger be inviting us over for a holiday dinner?"

Ginger tried to shrug her shoulderless arms. Ever since the very unfortunate events of Valentine's Day earlier that year, she had tried to forget the idea of finding a partner. "Your guess is as good as mine."

Ingrid opened her mouth to add something, but she was interrupted when Dave came dashing down the stairs with a panicked expression on his face. He looked here and there, his eyes wild. "A stranger approaches!" he shouted to everyone in the room. "He struck down the mouse outside—Chester! I saw it all from the balcony!"

"He—he struck down Chester?" inquired Ingrid. She tilted her head toward her husband. "Are we expecting any violent guests, my dear?"

Klaus said nothing, but his body shook and he clenched his claws. There was a forceful knock at the door, as if the stranger had manifested at the sound of Dave's foreboding words. Then there came a second series of knocks, and a third, each louder than the last.

"Klaus the Pretender!" shouted the unknown foe. "King of Sweetfort! You are called upon to answer for your misdeeds. Open this door! Your reckoning has come at last."

CHAPTER 2
Cowtown Counterstrike

If Ginger had been able to go pale, she was pretty sure she would have looked like an unfrosted sugar cookie by now. She looked around the room and saw that her friends were no better off: a haunted reminiscence hung in Klaus's eyes; Molasses had a quizzical look on his face and his whisk gripped between his arms; Ingrid's brow was furrowed at the rude interruption; Agapa glanced here and there with her bow in her hands, surveying all possible entrances for enemies; Reinhard moved in a clockwise circle, searching for a target to headbutt; Dave's eyes darted between the first floor and the staircase, depicting his inner debate as to where he should position himself; Horace, startled by the sudden noise, had squawked and fallen over, dropping his cane in the process.

"Any other enemies of yours we don't know about, Klaus?" Ginger asked, helping Horace stand. "Seems like you have a new one every few months."

"This isn't a new enemy," Klaus replied. He walked over to the war room and seized his paring knife, which was strapped to a popsicle stick display stand. "I've heard a voice like this once before."

"Open this door right now," demanded the stranger, "lest I break it down with brute force!"

"How did he get past the guards?" inquired Ingrid.

"Perhaps by appearing a friend," Agapa theorized.

Molasses grunted. "Stay back, Klaus. I'll handle this."

"No, my friend." The mouse took a breath and swung his knife through the air. Ginger remembered the last time he had wielded the blade, and how weak he had looked after months in prison. That weakness had passed, and Klaus was himself again—but now with a crown and superior swordsmanship. "He summoned *me*, and I must answer."

Ignoring the protestations of his wife and friends, he crossed the room and opened the door with his free paw. Ginger raced to his right side and Molasses to his left, and from there the foe could be clearly seen, illuminated by the outside Christmas lights. The rodent, standing on his hind legs, was so tall that his head nearly grazed the bottom of the balcony. Covering his body was a loose blue cloth—a hand towel, it seemed—that was also cupped around his head in a hooded fashion. Although he was concealed by the cloth, it was obvious that this creature was twice as broad as Klaus; he was a brute of a mouse who, in terms of sheer bulk, surpassed even Arthur, who had fallen during the Independence Day skirmish. His fur was mostly grey, but Ginger could see a deep brown hue between his ears that likely continued down his back. His eyes were as black as coal and his whiskers too short for his body. He seemed to carry no weapon of any kind, and Ginger thought he may not have needed one.

"Volsaph," Klaus muttered, extending a threatening glare. "Volsaph of the Voles of Cowtown. What brings you here? Clearly, it isn't to sit down to Harvest supper together."

"I will be with you in a moment, King Klaus!" Chester the butler announced, raising a paw from his place on the ground not a foot away from the front door. "The stranger crept up behind me and bludgeoned me with a walnut, the bugger. Rest assured, I will return to my duty as soon as I am able!"

Volsaph's eyes glowed in the dimness of Sweetfort, reflecting indoor and outdoor lights. He was staring not at Klaus but at the paring knife he held, deep hatred locked in his gaze. "You don't know how long I've waited for this day. Ever since you slew my brother with your cheap, craven maneuver, I've dreamed about the day that I would get revenge." As crowds began to gather behind him and listen, he seemed further egged on to deliver his monologue, and the volume of his voice increased. "My brother's death at your paws is what drove me to train tirelessly this past year and a half; I have become stronger than my brother ever was. And I will kill you for what you did to him and my family."

"Your brother?" Ginger mentally recited everything she knew about Klaus. "Volsaph....Are you the brother of Voliath? Klaus said he defeated your brother in combat."

Volsaph snarled at her and brandished a single arm. "Combat? Combat? There was no combat! Klaus didn't get within slashing distance of my brother. He picked up a rock and threw it, and by it my brother was slain. It was a fool's move—the move of a weakling, one who knew hand-to-hand combat would have gone unfavorably for him."

"Your brother challenged me," Klaus retorted, "and I answered the challenge. There were no rules of engagement; there was either victory or death."

"It was cowardly, and you know it!" Volsaph shook his head. "Your cowardice and disrespect for the rules of the duel have bereaved Volahmi and me of our beloved brother!"

Ginger snickered. "Volahmi? Like salami?"

"There were three of them," Klaus explained, turning his head toward her. "Three giantmice of the Voles of Cowtown: Voliath, Volsaph, and Volahmi. They made life a pain for King Shol and the mice of Sprinklevale, including myself and my kin. Daily ambushes at night on empty street corners; cruel traps out in the middle of the field; written mockeries of our slain. He speaks of *cowards*. Ha! His own know no other way but that of the craven."

"Very well!" Volsaph shouted. "Let's put your words to the test. Do you remember where you killed my brother?"

"Of course I do. The old stump near Mount Oniz and Lakeview Thicket, plumb center between Sprinkleton and Cowtown. A revered place among the mice of Sprinklevale, where Great Boris rested his weary whiskers during his sojourn."

"The very same. It is there that you will meet your end, Klaus. Later, at six o'clock at night as the humans tell it. There you must face me in hand-to-hand combat. No rocks. No distance between us except that of our blades."

"Six o'clock at night?" Ginger's arms flew to her face. "That's when we planned on having our Harvest supper!"

"Harvest supper is canceled," said Volsaph. He turned to the listening crowd and waved a single paw toward them. "Do you hear that, Mice of Sweetfort? Your Harvest supper and all your festivities are canceled! I call upon you, and upon the cookies of your dear alliance, to watch as your king falls before me. The Voles of Cowtown will be watching, as well. If Klaus dies, you and your alliance must join us. If I die, then the voles will join you. These are my terms."

"Don't do it, Klaus!" Ginger implored him. "You have no obligation to agree to this. You defeated Voliath fair and square, and the Fur-Crumb Alliance needs you!"

Ingrid came up behind Klaus and touched his arm. "I'd prefer you not entertain this scoundrel, dear husband...but you are the king, and I trust you'll do what is right."

Klaus glanced at each of his friends, and then lastly at Ingrid, with a variety of contemplative expressions. He gazed out at his foe and at the mice of his kingdom. With a small sigh, he lowered his head and stabbed the end of his knife into the floor. "I accept your terms, Volsaph. We will meet you at Great Boris's Stump at six o'clock in the evening, and there you and I will do battle. Under one condition."

Volsaph turned back to him and smirked. "Name it, coward."

"You inflict no harm on my wife, Ginger, Molasses, or any of my fellow mice or cookie allies. The Fur-Crumb Alliance remains safe, no matter what happens."

The brutish mouse stared at him, unblinking. "Fine, fine. Agreed." He shrugged. "I would worry more about my own hide, if I were you, but do as you will. I will be preparing for our duel...and to finally deliver retribution for what you did to my brother."

"I took no joy in killing Voliath," Klaus informed him. "Sincerely, I mean that. But he was a threat to the vale and irreverent to everything we hold dear. For me, there was no choice in the matter."

"Nor is there a choice for me." Volsaph waved at him and at everyone else indoors. "I'll see you all later. You best brace yourselves for what you're about to experience."

He turned away, walked past Chester the butler (who had finally managed to stand), and disappeared into the dark of the tunnel. The crowd exchanged anxious chitters and made an occasional glance at Klaus as if they expected him to make a grand speech; or perhaps they were simply concerned for their king, and were wishing that such an ill omen had not befallen him on the day of gratitude. The latter sentiment belonged to Ginger. *This wasn't the way this day was supposed to go*! she thought. *Klaus was supposed to enjoy time with his loved ones, and now he very well could be dead in twelve hours. Why can't things ever go according to plan? Why are we doomed to suffer every time there's a holiday?*

All eyes were on Klaus as he sauntered from the doorway to the war room and examined a set of armor resting on a display case. The helmet, pauldrons, gorget, cuirass, gauntlets, tassets, and greaves appeared to have been fashioned from a soda can, and each piece had been spraypainted gold. *He means to wear that tonight*, Ginger realized. Upon closer inspection, she observed that the armor was double-layered—a great defense against a slash and a fair defense against a bludgeon, but not very effective against a stab. She was confident that Volsaph would discover this weakness within seconds and exploit it, using his extended reach to thrust his blade through his foe's armor before Klaus could even attempt his first blow. Ginger could not allow it. There had to be something she could do.

Ingrid went to her husband and stood between him and the suit of armor. She placed a paw on his crown. "I think we should consider our options, dear. There is too much at stake here. You are the most skilled warrior I've ever seen, but the fire you had within you when you faced Voliath is no longer there. That's not because you have grown weak; it's because you know that Volsaph only seeks to avenge his brother, and he does not mock our friends and our values the way Voliath did. This is a different kind of battle altogether."

Klaus nodded. "I have no desire to kill him, Ingrid, but I must. Fire within or no, his victory would mean the subjugation of our kingdom—every mouse who has found freedom and peace here, and every cookie who has benefited from the Alliance. I must fight for the vale."

"What if we were to set a trap for the Voles of Cowtown? You know, we all get there hours early and hide in the bushes, then ambush them when they get there."

"They'll be expectin' a trap, muh queen," said Horace. "The voles've been at this a long time. They prolly already have guards posted in every surrounding bush as we speak."

"There are no other options, Ingrid," Klaus said to her. "I must defeat Volsaph in battle. I'm sorry."

Molasses hummed so loudly to himself that everyone looked at him. He exchanged a glance with both Agapa and Reinhard, and they nodded at him. Ginger could not deny that she felt a little jealous at being excluded from the "inner circle" that was Molasses, Agapa, and Reinhard. As she had heard it, the trio had spent weeks together looking for her prior to Independence Day and had developed a close bond. Even Dave was closer to the inner circle than she was, and he was a relative newcomer. She *was* aware enough to see that the trio apparently shared the same thought, but for all she knew, they could have telepathically agreed that a tomato was better classified as a vegetable than as a fruit. No, that could not be it.

"Tell them, Molasses," Agapa said.

Ingrid's eyes narrowed curiously. "Tell us what?"

Molasses sighed and stepped into the center of the room. "As you all know, I have been leading the cookies of Mount Oniz in training exercises so that they are better equipped to fight our enemies when the day comes. But knowing your enemy is every bit as important as having the martial edge over your enemy. I'm sure you remember my story: how Tanas deceived me, and how I succumbed to his temptation. As a way to make amends, I have studied deceit as a strategy, and I have taught the Cookies of Theo to do the very same. Reinhard, Agapa, and I agree that Volsaph is deceiving you, Klaus. The extent of that deceit I don't know, but I *do* know that he is neglecting to tell you something very important."

Klaus's ears fidgeted with interest. "What do you think he's hiding, Molasses?"

"I don't know him, so I can't even begin to guess. But think about it, all of you. Klaus killed Volsaph's brother well over a year ago. Why does he come to our doorstep now? He claims to have been training—that now he's 'ready' to face Klaus. Why now? And he seemed intent on drawing a crowd and getting everyone's attention. Klaus, he wants your entire kingdom out there at Great Boris's Stump. Firstly, that leaves your every follower vulnerable. Secondly, that leaves Sweetfort vulnerable."

"That's all true," said Klaus. "So what do you suggest?"

"Have three-quarters of your kingdom and three-quarters of the cookies from Mount Oniz come out to watch the duel. If there is an ambush, then at least you stand a fighting chance. Leave the other quarter back here. If the voles try to take your kingdom, the few here may be able to hold them off, or at least have an easier time of escape."

Klaus grinned. "You have adopted quite the tactical mind, my friend."

Molasses attempted a mirthful chuckle, but the circumstances made it sound dry and forced. "I've learned from a fairly brilliant mouse, who also happens to be a king."

"And what are *we* going to do?" Ginger asked no one in particular. "We're part of the Fur-Crumb Alliance now, so we can't just stand by and do nothing."

"We will do no such thing," Agapa assured her, smiling. "If I am succeeding in reading Molasses's mind, then he has another plan for us."

"Indeed!" exclaimed Reinhard, hopping and then hovering in the air. "We make for Cowtown!"

Ginger turned to look at her brother. "We make for Cowtown?"

Molasses gave her a single nod. "Into the heart of the vole kingdom, to collect intel and to compromise their defenses. They'll never see it coming."

"I can't ask that of you, my dear friends," Klaus told them, leaving the war room and going to them. He looked at Ginger. "I know what Cowtown means to the Cookies of Theo: it's the place where Tanas fled after his defeat at

Christmastime. You wouldn't just be going into the heart of vole territory; you would be approaching the one who corrupted you at the beginning. That's too much to ask."

"Like Molasses said, they'll never see it coming," Ginger assured him. She did her best to exude the same confidence she had seen in her brother. "We'll be fine, Klaus. I already have an idea of how we'll bypass their defenses."

"How?" The mouse's eyes darted here and there anxiously.

"Our favorite tactic, of course: subterfuge."

Ginger's strike team was comprised of six members: herself, Molasses, Agapa, Reinhard, Dave, and Horace. Providentially, half of their merry band was capable of flying and moving faster than those bound to the land, and so it was decided that the "flyers" would bear the "walkers" through the air—using spools of fishing line generously supplied by Klaus—until they had reached Cowtown, as this would save on time. Molasses sat atop Reinhard, leading the group; Agapa held a string to which Ginger was attached; Dave held a string to which Horace was attached. The old mouse had volunteered to come along, as he had knowledge of Cowtown, its inhabitants, and its ways. Like Ginger, he also had a knack for diplomacy; but Ginger, being something of a pacifist, recognized the worth of having a diplomat who could threaten the swift wrath of Klaus if the situation called for it. The only time she had ever threatened anyone was when she had told Molasses that she would kick him out of their gingerbread house if he did not clean up after himself, and he had just laughed in her face and fallen asleep surrounded by filth. The pile of filth was still sitting in his room, last time she checked—not that she checked twice a day or anything.

After nearly two hours of flying, Horace directed them to turn east by several degrees to avoid Great Boris's Stump. Once it was within view, Ginger noticed that it looked like any other stump, if not a bit broader; around it were several shrubs and grass that were developing a dark green shade, enlivened by the sporadic rains of autumn. Molasses, hanging on to Reinhard's antlers with the end of one arm, swept his looking glass from his belt with his free arm and raised it to one eye with some difficulty. He announced to the group that there was not a vole in sight, neither on the grass nor in the bushes. Ginger thought that this was suspicious, for the Voles of Cowtown were surely intelligent enough to secure the area and dissuade the Mice of Sweetfort from attempting an ambush or some other ploy. There was also the unsettling possibility that the voles had not yet left their kingdom, and Ginger and her group would be sneaking into a fort rife with enemies.

They had nearly made it to the western side of Lakeview Thicket, as the locals called it, when Agapa pointed out a structure to the north. Although it was too far away to be seen clearly, Ginger could tell that it was made of flat wood, unmarred by holes or pockets of any kind, and that it stood about the height of the average human. Agapa rose a bit higher in the air to get a better view, and from there, Ginger noticed that the "structure" was actually two wooden walls running parallel to each other, with a small gap or runway between them. These walls stretched some way across the field from west to east and disappeared into the forest. She wondered what they might be; she had never seen them from Mount Oniz, and she thought that the wood looked *fresh,* somehow. Maybe the Sprinkletonians were starting on a road that would connect the town to the woods to better access certain resources.

Before she knew it, Sprinklevale was behind her, and the team had entered lands unknown to the Cookies of Theo. Lakeview Thicket, which cupped the eastern side of the vale, was not wide by any human standard, but to a cookie, it might as well have been the Amazon. Ginger was accustomed to the woods of Mount Oniz, where the trees were dispersed far apart and whereby natural paths were established; here the trees nearly hugged one another, their branches tangling in a beautiful but chaotic jade tapestry. The forest seemed to her an impenetrable film that separated one world from another, and suddenly she felt afraid, more afraid than she had in months. Every comfort she had ever known was far behind her, and uncharted territory lay ahead—a place where foreign inhabitants dwelled, and where her powerful enemy brooded. Even the rocks and carpet of the forest appeared altogether alien, further confirmation that there was nothing of Sprinklevale in this world except the cookies who had breached it.

She turned her eyes ahead to Molasses, who was surveilling the landscape for the presence of unwanted attention. Despite her countless sisterly frustrations with him, she was proud that he had finally managed to move beyond the guilt of his past failures and embraced his gifting. He had become an invaluable asset to both the Cookies of Theo and the Mice of Sweetfort; seeing his change over time brought her a realization that it is sometimes the most reprobate offenders who, after being changed by Mr. Theo, bring about the most profound good. Molasses, a former pawn of Tanas intent on taking life, was now leading the charge into a foreign land to preserve life. If that was not evidence of her maker's guiding hand in the lives of those he loved, Ginger was not sure what was.

Within the hour the trees abruptly vanished, and here began what appeared to be an endlessly broad cluster of rolling hills, interrupted by a solitary road to the south that linked Sprinkleton to Cowtown. The world came alive with scattered cows mooing and chewing their cud, armies of dragonflies loitering along the hillsides, bees moving from flower to flower beneath the morning light, and birds flitting across the cloud-specked sky. Ginger was pleased to see that here all traces of the yellow grass of summer had faded, and that everything was healthy and vibrant and green, a testament to the more frequent rains of the wild. She was sure that within a month's time, with the inevitable colder weather, a thin layer of snow would dress every slope, and children from town would find their way into adult-free zones where they could build their snowmen or have their snowball fights. Mount Oniz would again find its pines, bushes, and earth brushed with frost, and the homes of Sprinkleton would be aglow with string lights. Some of the more festive families had already purchased their Christmas trees and erected their lawn decorations, giving passersby a foretaste of the most wonderful time of the year. A smile stretched across Ginger's face, but it disappeared as quickly as it had come when she remembered their current purpose and her best friend's peril.

After about four hours of travel, with the midmorning sun beaming down upon them, the travelers alighted on a hill looming high above the northwestern border of Cowtown, and from there it could be seen in its fullness. Immediately evident was the difference in the colors of roofs and house siding; whereas Sprinkleton was known for its bright reds and tans, Cowtown seemed to consist primarily of rusts and dark browns. Cowtown also dwarfed Sprinkleton in size, perhaps ten times over, and whatever could be found in the latter was multiplied in the former: four gas stations rather than one, ten restaurants rather than two, one hundred moving cars rather than thirty. As far as Ginger was concerned, this was the largest town in the world—though she heard Shanghai was pretty big, too.

"Okay, we're here," Molasses announced as he hopped off Reinhard's back. "What's our next move, Horace?"

"Our spies say that King Chisha's fortress is where it's always been: inside the garage o' the Hoarder of Bovine Lane. He's an elderly chap that only moves from his living room to his kitchen and back again, givin' the voles free reign over his garage."

Reinhard gave Horace a quizzical look. "And King Chisha is...."

"The king o' the voles."

"Ah, yes. Of course." He turned to Agapa and dropped his voice to a whisper. "Too many kings to keep track of."

"The house'll be easy to find: it sits on the northmost corner o' the street, an' all manner of destroyed cardboard boxes an' weatherworn bins sit in the front yard. Findin' King Chisha's fortress should also be easy. Enterin' it undetected? Not so much."

"I can see the house from here," said Molasses, holding his looking glass to his eye. "Sister, do you want to take a look?"

Ginger hobbled across the moist grass and took the device from him. She raised it and pointed it to the northeast, and the house showed up right away; besides the boxes and bins, the grass in the yard was also dried and unkempt, and the roots of a single tree in the center lifted the ground unevenly. "The garage door is closed, and so is the side door, which must also lead into the garage. Good golly! How are we going to get inside?"

"There be openin's on the right side o' the main garage door an' under the side door," Horace explained, "but both be closely watched. We'd be killed or 'rrested on sight."

Ginger gave Molasses a mournful look. "We didn't think this through, did we, Brother?"

Horace placed both paws on top of his cherry stem cane and leaned heavily on it. "There's a third route, one not so closely guarded. Under the eaves on the north side o' the garage is a attic vent covered with—what do they call it again?—*low-grade wire mesh*, partly destroyed years ago. We've our rat cousins to thank for that." He tittered at the mention of the rats, a joke that went over Ginger's head and, clearly, over the heads of the other cookies. "Anywho, King Chisha's soldiers don' hang around the opening o' that vent, as birds go in an' out through the day. If we can ensure the coast is clear an' post someone up there to ferry the rest o' us into the attic, we should be able to 'pproach the fortress from above; we might even get the jump on a lone soldier in the attic an' get the information we need."

"Birds go in and out of the attic all day?" Ginger let out a nervous laugh. "Do birds have a fondness for sweets— cookies, to be exact?"

"The other day, I saw a boy throw a chocolate chip cookie to a crow," replied Dave. "The crow snatched it up without a second thought."

"Yes," said Agapa. "Birds will eat cookies if they are hungry enough, and if there is naught else nearby that is desirable."

"Birds aren't picky eaters," said Horace. "They love most anything, an' cookies be no exception."

"I love this plan," Ginger muttered. "I love it so much."

Horace tittered again. "Fear not, Ms. Ginger. Long as we're watchful, careful, an' quick, we should be fine." He squinted in the direction of their destination. "Right now, *quickness* is most important. It's well past ten o'clock already; a little over seven hours until muh king is expected at Great Boris's Stump."

"Then let's get moving," Molasses urged them. "If there's a plot to be uncovered, we must uncover it *now*."

CHAPTER 3
Famished Feathered Friends

Ginger watched the wingless Reinhard float up to the attic vent after Agapa and Dave. The Cupid cookies flittered through the opening, vanished for a few seconds, and then reappeared and lifted their bows in the air—a sign that there was no immediate danger. Reinhard entered soon thereafter, and just a few moments later the trio were threading a fishing line through the wire mesh and down toward the base of the wall. Ginger and the others were waiting in a strip of faux red bark that framed the front lawn; they had positioned themselves between two misshapen shrubs to avoid being seen by drivers on the busy street. The team had managed to fly high over the street without being spotted (as far as she knew), but being ferried slowly along the wall of a house in broad daylight would be another situation entirely. It was decided that they would pull one individual into the attic at a time, for even the three strong cookies would struggle to pull up their three friends expeditiously. It did not help that Ginger had gained a approximately five ounces in the past two months, a fact over which she had been groaning to Molasses for a week, and a fact that Molasses vehemently argued was not, in fact, a fact.

They agreed that Horace, the most aged of the crew, should be lifted first; then followed Ginger, and finally Molasses. It was not the lifting that took long, but rather the waiting for all traffic on the road to clear, and Ginger was shocked to see the sun approaching its zenith by the time the entire group had made it into the attic. Once they had walked a short distance from the vent, they huddled up, exchanged a quick nod, and peered out into the dark until their eyes had adjusted. Narrow, beech-colored wood beams loomed overhead, extending into the unseeable distance, birds' nests wedged in many corners where a horizontal beam intersected with one that was vertical. The floor looked like cotton candy, with pink insulation blanketing the ceiling. Interrupting the insulation were additional beams that would serve as the cookies' walkway; at one point several of these beams met and were topped with a broad, flat piece of wood. A massive grey machine, whirring calmly, crested this platform, and around it lay four or five rat traps. Ginger could see that the peanut butter sitting in the bait troughs of the traps had hardened with age.

"That's the way, over there," Horace whispered, gesturing toward the machine. "There's a pocket in the ceiling that opens into the garage. Ord'narily, the voles stay away from that area 'cause the rat traps pose a danger. Such traps ain't a problem for us mice, usually, as we be too small to set 'em off; but these voles're *hefty*, you understand me? They've eaten one too many kabocha squashes, get my drift? They're *plump*, got it? If one of 'em touches that peanut butter, it's lights out."

"But I see others on the walkways, scouring the area," said Dave. "We're not alone up here."

"And that's where the 'careful' and 'watchful' part o' the plan come in." Horace looked here and there, and as Ginger followed his gaze, she noticed that the nearest guards had turned their backs and were walking away from them, toward the perimeter of the attic. "Okay, now! Follow me."

The mouse, who was fairly plump himself, waddled across the wood stage on which he had been standing and began to balance on one of the beams that reached toward the machine. Ginger was next, and then Agapa (scanning the left) and Dave (scanning the right), and Reinhard staring straight ahead, and Molasses as the rearguard with his mace drawn. As they penetrated deeper into the heart of the expansive room, several more guards were revealed, bringing the total to about a dozen. Ginger clenched every crumb within her as she balanced along, fearing that the slightest misstep would alert her foes to her presence. Being seen was not a major concern to her, for she knew well the limitations of mice; but their hearing was heightened, catching sounds that other creatures might miss. If she took a loud, careless step or tripped on a poorly hammered nail, then there was nothing stopping the voles from circling her and turning her into a five-course meal. She was confident that they were nowhere near as merciful as the Colony Behind the Cabinets!

On and on they went into the ever-thickening darkness, each step separating them further from the light that shone through the attic vents. Fortunately, they were also distancing themselves further from the voles as they drew nearer to the whirring machine. Ginger examined the trap-laden platform and noticed that it was remarkably free of mouse droppings; she suspected that it had taken just one rotund vole sticking his snout where it should not have been to teach the others to steer clear of the traps, no matter how tantalizing the peanut butter they contained. There *were* older, larger droppings, probably from the same rats who had granted them convenient access to the attic through the wire mesh of the vent. Ginger had never seen a rat in her life, and based on Klaus's harrowing description of the demons, she did not intend to.

Although she had no lungs to speak of, she let out a huge (and quiet) breath once the group had reached the platform. The machine was almost a perfect cube, barring an indentation along the top on the side facing them, which was spotted with several blinking buttons; also on the side facing them, about halfway down the surface, was a strip of metal pocked with holes, and behind it was a red glow that seemed to emit heat. Horace pointed to the other side of the machine, and there Ginger saw an opening in the platform and the inner wall of the cavity that plunged down into the garage below. *Just a little further*, she told herself. *Just a little further, and you'll be safe...in a vole fortress, surrounded by enemies. Come on, Ginger, you can do this*!

She followed Horace onto the platform and felt an immediate spike in anxiety, for once she had left behind the wooden beam, she stepped into a spotlight that filtered down through a turbine vent above. Mice were known for their poor vision, but she thought that even *they* could see a band of trespassers highlighted in the brightest part of the attic. She took one step, two steps, three; all was silent, all was going smoothly, and she was less than a foot away from the opening. Horace wove between two rat traps, and behind him Ginger and Agapa followed closely. Then there was a sound—a loud *crack* that reverberated through the attic—that must have been the wood settling or contracting from the cold, and Dave was startled. He nocked an arrow and dropped back to scan his surroundings, and in the process he careened into Reinhard, knocking him back...onto a rat trap.

The rat trapped snapped shut with ferocity, narrowly missing Reinhard; the reindeer cookie shouted and leapt away, only to land directly onto a second trap and set it off. This one also missed him, but he was so panicked that he shouted once more, bounded high into the air, and landed onto the platform with a loud *thump*. Then he fell over.

In seconds, the voles, as plump as they were, sped at them from every direction, and Ginger knew there was nothing they could do. If they were, in an attempt to escape, to drop down into the garage below, the guards would follow and alert the entire fortress to their presence. If they made a run for it, back toward the outdoors, they would be struck down. All they could do was remain in place and hope that they were not killed on sight. Ginger went to Molasses's side and put her arms around him, and she could feel the obvious contrast between her trembling features and his unflinching resolve. His whisk was still held between his arms, but he held it at an angle, as though he did not think he would need it. *I wish I could be so fearless and confident*, she thought. *Molasses seems ready for anything, and yet here I am, cowering per usual. How does he do it?*

The twenty or so voles, with their light brown fur coats and their significant bulk, reached the platform and formed a circle around the group. Most were garbed in sandpaper squares that were layered upon one another like the armor of samurai, the armor primarily protecting their upper bodies and thighs; their heads, short tails, and diminutive paws were left uncovered. Each vole held a bow comprised of a single twig and a broken rubber band, and against each bowstring rested a toothpick aimed at the interlopers. Fear and curiosity played upon the countenances of several voles, and it was only then that Ginger realized many of them had never seen a living cookie before. She hoped that would somehow work to their advantage.

A prominent vole, and the only one donning a sandpaper helmet, pushed his way between a few of his peers to the east and stepped into the fullness of the light. At first there was a look of indignation in his eyes, but when he had examined each member of the group, he appeared surprised. His muscles softening, he removed his helmet and held it at his side. "Molasses?" he said, blinking. "Agapa? Reinhard?"

Ginger's mouth dropped open. "Brother, how on earth does this ninja warrior know your name?"

Molasses stared forward, incredulous. "Bahar?"

"What—what are you doing here?" asked the vole. "It's not safe for you to be here."

"Bahar," said one of the voles nearest him, "what are these—things? And how do you know them?"

Bahar looked to his allies and gestured for them to lower their weapons, a command that they quickly followed. Ginger could tell that the rodent "wore his heart on his sleeve," as the humans put it; every thought and emotion that he felt as he considered his words displayed on his face. "Several months ago, days before we were preparing for the attack on King Shol, I was making my way back to Cowtown with the latest intel on Shol's forces and fortifications. This trio—Molasses, Reinhard, and Agapa—spotted me." He nodded toward Reinhard. "This one here headbutted me and sent me flying a full yard."

Ginger looked at the reindeer cookie with disapproval. "Really, Reinhard?"

"That was *my* reaction," Bahar continued, "until I understood the reason for it. They believed me to be allied with Shol, and they assumed I might know where Molasses's sister, Ginger, was being kept. I assume that's you?"

"You assume right."

"Then you found her," Bahar said to Molasses with a small smile. "I'm glad to know that the information I shared helped in your search."

"We had to corroborate it first, which is another story entirely," replied Molasses, "but yes, your intel proved to be helpful."

Bahar stared at the cookie for about five seconds and let out a long sigh. "I was very forgiving last time, even after the reindeer knocked me down. I was patient with the three of you. But now you're here, and not just the trio I met; there is also this mouse, whom I recognize as a follower of Klaus. I'm under strict orders to apprehend strangers and neutralize any mice who come from Sweetfort."

Something pressed at Ginger from within: an urge, an understanding that it was time for her to speak up. She left Molasses's side and stepped forward. "Sir, please take a moment to listen to me before you make any decisions. You seem to be a reasonable vole; I ask that you give me the chance to explain why we're here. Then...well, if it doesn't satisfy you, you can do with us as you will."

The light in his eyes told her that she had at least piqued his curiosity. "Very well. Go on, explain yourself."

"May I start by asking you something?"

"Fine, go ahead," he answered, wrinkling his snout.

"Have you ever met Klaus?"

"No, I've never had the displeasure. Nor have any among us here, because we're all under a year old, and Klaus hasn't had dealings with the voles since summer of last year—or so we're told. Nearly a year and a half ago."

"Well, Klaus is my best friend. Shortly after I was enlivened by Mr. Theo, I was commissioned to go down into Sprinkleton."

"Mr. Theo was your maker," said Bahar, nodding. "And what was the reason for your commission?"

"I had gone astray," replied Molasses. "I was enticed by my desires and made a series of bad decisions that led me into the heart of Sprinkleton. Ginger's objective was to persuade me to leave behind my wicked way and return to our creator on Mount Oniz."

"I was so...*scared*, Bahar," said Ginger. "Terrified. I had never been down to Sprinkleton before. It was overwhelming, and I felt so...alone. But as I searched through one of the homes for my brother, I became acquainted with Klaus, who was then acting as an unofficial king over the Colony Behind the Cabinets. I say 'unofficial,' because he didn't want the title, and he only served in a position of leadership because the other mice insisted on following him."

"That—that can't be true," said one of Bahar's mice. "We were told he declared himself king around Christmastime last year."

"No, not at all," responded Molasses. "Even the crown he wears now, he was hesitant to accept. Klaus is a willing hero but a reluctant king; he doesn't consider himself worthy of a crown."

"That's a common trait with the best of kings," said Ginger, "not that I've met many of them. I did meet King Shol, and he was a bit of a lummox."

"On that we agree," laughed Bahar. "But the lummox is dead, and only two colonies remain in the region."

"For now." Ginger sulked as she pictured Klaus in combat, fighting for his life against a much larger foe. "This morning, Volsaph of Cowtown came to Klaus's doorstep and challenged him to a duel. Of course, Klaus accepted, and even now he readies himself. There's a chance that he'll be the victor, but there's also a chance—small as it may be—that Volsaph will kill *him*. This hero, this reluctant king, and my closest friend—he could lose his life today. And whoever wins will be awarded the allegiance of the opposing colony."

"Those were the terms of the agreement, at least," Molasses explained. "But I suspect that there's more to this than meets the eye. I think Volsaph has something up his sleeve."

"So...what?" Bahar appeared indignant. "You came all this way in hopes of confirming a hunch?"

"It is more than a hunch, Bahar!" Reinhard declared. "Molasses is trained in the art of lie-detection, and his cookie sense is tingling."

"Please don't talk about my tingling cookie sense," muttered Molasses.

"Understood, my friend!"

Bahar looked at Molasses, then at Ginger, and then at the platform beneath him. He clasped his claws behind his back and began to pace, whispering something to himself. All eyes were glued to him, a fact that seemed to increase the visible stress that showed on his brow. Some of his followers shot a glance at each other and exchanged a few questioning words, as if they wondered what he might do or say. Finally, after about a full minute had passed, he stopped and turned his attention to Molasses.

"The conspiracy runs deeper than you know," he said, and Ginger saw something new in the vole's eyes; it was a look of resignation, as though he had accepted the treasonous and traitorous words that were about to leave his mouth. The terror on the faces of the other guards only further testified to this. "There's something important I have to tell you concerning Volsaph's plan, although it's not really his to begin with; however, I don't think this is the place for it. We're far too exposed out here."

"Is there a safe haven where we might discuss this?" asked Agapa.

The vole nodded. "On the other side of the attic, to the east, to the north, and then to the east again. We have a room against the roof with a window looking out over the neighborhood. Our chief strategists use it from time to time, but today it's vacant. It'll be safe from prying ears and eyes."

"Are you sure you want to do this, Bahar?" inquired Molasses. "You're putting yourself at great risk. You *could* pretend you never saw us, and we could collect the information another way."

"That's another topic for discussion. I—I'm sorry, not here. We will speak openly over at the war room." He stiffened and turned his attention to the guards standing at the edge of the platform. "My fellow voles, I know I've broken protocol, but I ask you to trust me as you have these past few months. Continue with your appointed routes, and I'll address you shortly."

The voles responded with a dubious salute before splitting off into each quadrant of the attic. Bahar motioned for Ginger's group to follow him, and together they crossed the single beam stretching to the northern side of the house, the pink lake of insulation bordering them on the left and right. At one point Ginger observed that there was a patch of insulation missing and a small hole in the ceiling, granting a view of the eastern interior of the resident's garage. Against the wall stood three blue, overturned storage bins; the one in the center was massive, and the two on either side of it almost half as large. Empty clay flowerpots rested upside-down on top of each corner of the bins, and two vole guards were posted on each pot. The top of the bins appeared to be the battlement of the castle, and the flowerpots watchtowers. The voles had chewed entrances and exits into the coarse material, having even fashioned a grand entrance in the external wall of the middle bin, and having made a walkway leading to this entrance between moat-like glue boards that circled the center castle. *There must be at least three hundred mice living in there*, Ginger realized, panic sweeping through her. *That's more than three times the number of Klaus's mice in Sweetfort. If they were to ambush him, it would be ugly, even with some of our cookies there to help. Do the voles know that? Is that what Bahar is getting ready to tell us?*

They turned north and scurried along a beam for about a minute before making a right turn and facing east. The "war room," hugging the place where the eastern slope of the roof met with the beams and the walls below, was contained in a glorified shoebox. A semicircle entrance had been chewed or clawed into the western surface, and two sets of toothpick rapiers crisscrossed on either side of the portal. Bahar led them into the box, and they were surprised by a blast of light that filled the room. Ginger saw, as her frosting eyes adjusted to the brightness, that there was no eastern wall of the shoebox; its wall was the wire mesh of an attic vent, which presented a panorama of much of Cowtown. The brown roofs were refulgent beneath the late morning sun, as were the rusty bricks of which most of the homes were crafted. Inside the room an oval table, looking to be an artificial wood bookmark of some kind, was mounted on a black whetstone. The lids of soda bottles, meant to be chairs, surrounded the table.

"Have a seat," Bahar entreated them, setting his helmet down on the table. "I think you'll need it."

"What's King Chisha up to?" Horace demanded, sounding grumpy. Although the others sat down, he declined the offer and instead leaned on his cane. "I'm hopin' you'll explain why he sends out a champion rather than face Klaus in battle 'imself."

"This plan is supported by King Chisha," Bahar explained, "but it didn't originate with him."

"If he supports it, it might as well've originated with him!" Horace spat. "Volsaph called Klaus a coward. Bah! Only a coward sends out a warrior to fight his battles for him. Klaus's never asked anyone to fight a battle he wouldn't fight 'imself."

"Listen to me," said Bahar, "and listen closely. There will be no battle today."

Dave started. "It is already scheduled. Six o'clock in the evening."

"That is the time that the Alliance will arrive at Great Boris's Stump, but there will be no battle. Allow me—allow me to tell the story from the beginning." He sighed and turned to the window to gaze out at the dozens of houses. "A farmer moved into town just before the beginning of this year. He purchased a plot of land not far from here and had a house and barn constructed. The man planted fruits and vegetables of all kinds; even those that had no business existing in this climate were thriving. Acres and acres of his land expand to the northwest of town, filled with more produce than anyone, even a town as large as Cowtown, could consume in a lifetime. And so, after getting the lay of the land earlier this year, the voles ventured onto his property and started stealing some of his produce. This went on for a couple of months, and we were quite successful. But one night, when a group went out to the land, the farmer was waiting for them. He turned on a flashlight as they were in the middle of their act of theft, and they were filled with terror. But the man did...nothing. He just stood there and smiled at them. He even held his hand toward his produce, as if offering it to the trespassers. Then he shut off his flashlight and turned away, and the voles, stunned but thankful, collected as much food as they could carry.

"This unspoken alliance went on for months...but it didn't *remain* unspoken. Early in July, almost five months ago, it's said that a group of cookies showed up outside our castle and asked if they could speak with 'the one in charge.'"

"Cookies?" Molasses asked him, wide-eyed. "Did you meet them? Did you see who they were? What they looked like?"

"Not personally, no. Nor did my guards. This is only a second-hand story." He looked at Molasses, and his face tightened with concentration. "But I was told some of their names. Clove, Limerence, and Frostina...not names that one would easily forget."

There was a change in the atmosphere at the mention of these names, and everyone shifted in their seats with discomfort. Ginger believed that she was the most stricken of the lot, by far. After all, it was Clove who had shouted at and tortured her in Shol's Funland around Independence Day, and who had left her with a hole in her arm that she still bore. It was Limerence who had fired a "love dart" into her back on Valentine's Eve, forcing her to develop an infatuation with Klaus. She had never really been close with Frostina, but the snowwoman cookie had once looked up to her and regarded Molasses with respect; now she was gone, having left Mount Oniz with Crumble, Anise, and Glacia, bitter about the way Molasses had handled...well, pretty much everything while Ginger had been in prison. The Fur-Crumb Alliance had learned nothing of the cookies' whereabouts after the Independence Day skirmish, which made the idea that they had migrated to Cowtown believable. She felt something drop where her heart might have been. *They're here. Our enemies are here. Just how close to them are we right now, anyway?*

"I see that you're familiar with these names," said Bahar.

"Yes, we know them," mumbled Agapa.

Bahar fleeced one of his whiskers. "The looks on your faces tell me that you didn't endorse the expedition of those cookies. They came here of their own will."

"Sir, what do those traitors have to do with the farmer and the Voles of Cowtown?" asked Ginger.

The mouse paused to look at her. "Have you noticed that cookies seem to have no issue communicating with mice? Of course you have; that's what your alliance is all about. And you were made by Mr. Theo, with whom you can also communicate—or with whom you *used* to communicate, as the rumor goes. I hear that he doesn't speak to you so much nowadays."

"He speaks in other ways," said Molasses. "Not with his audible voice, not usually, but through letters he has given us."

"My point is that you cookies have the ability to speak to both mice—or rodents—and humans. Have you ever seen a *mouse* try to speak to a human? It's pathetic. It's like all the human can hear is squeaking or something. Or maybe all they hear is insults, because they sure seem intent on killing us or removing us from their homes.

"We can speak to you. You can speak to humans. And that's how our unspoken alliance with the farmer became one that was spoken; Clove and his friends became our interpreters, middlemen making our words known to the farmer, and vice-versa. And through the connection of these 'traitors,' as you refer to them, a bond has been made. Trust has developed between the man and the voles.

"About a month ago, the farmer summoned some of our leaders and the cookies and expressed some significant concerns. He shared that the ecosystem of this region is delicate and can be easily thrown off balance, and with Thanksgiving coming up, there would likely be a near-extermination of turkeys at the hands of hunters. As I have heard it told, he really put on quite a show; he wept, he trembled, he sulked. With this display, and with his claim that the turkeys were lower in number than they had been in years, he persuaded my fellow voles—with the cookies as his mouthpiece—to be on the lookout for the feathered creatures. He told us to make the turkeys an offer to stay in his barn until the holiday season was over. And so, since the end of October, we have been meeting with turkeys in the woods, on the side of the road, out in the field—anywhere—and telling them about the farmer's barn. Most of them have wholeheartedly agreed to the offer, and we have led them to the barn, where the farmer has welcomed them with open arms. Only...." Bahar let out a sorrowful grunt, and Ginger could see tears in his eyes. "Only, that's not the end of the story."

"Did the farmer slaughter the turkeys and eat them all himself?" inquired Reinhard.

"No, he didn't eat them; it's even worse. He has not *fed* them."

Agapa looked furious. "He has *starved* them?"

Bahar nodded hesitantly. "Yes, yes he has. He has starved them for *weeks*. It must have been his plan from the beginning, but he didn't tell us. His goal was to starve the turkeys and, when the time was right, to release them and feed them at last."

Horace swallowed. "Feed them *what*?"

"With mice, and with the cookies of the Fur-Crumb Alliance." Bahar shook his head and avoided eye contact with everyone in the room. "The challenge was getting Klaus and all his followers in one place at one time. It was decided that we would create a ruse: the duel. Our leaders asked Volsaph to fabricate a desire for vengeance for the death of his brother. They promised that if he agreed to their plan, not only would Volsaph get the satisfaction of watching Klaus die, but he would also be granted his own corner of the farmer's land and would be entitled to any produce contained within."

"Why would the Voles of Cowtown agree to this?" Molasses asked, writhing with anger. "Once you learned that the farmer was starving the turkeys, why didn't you all just rebel against him and free your feathered friends?"

"That's what *I* wanted to do...but I have no voice here, not one that matters. The only authority I hold is over the guards who patrol this attic." Bahar placed a paw against the wall and looked out at the town again. "Greed is a very real temptation, Molasses. Do you know what it's like to have someone offer you everything you have ever wanted? Do you know what it's like to be promised that you'll never lack anything ever again, and that you'll be content for the rest of your days?"

Ginger huffed and crossed her arms. "We *do* know what that's like. We know *exactly* what it's like."

Molasses nodded at his sister. "Bahar, tell us—what is the name of this farmer?"

He looked back and forth between them. "He is called Tanas."

The cookies went silent, and even Horace placed a paw against his forehead as if he might faint. Ginger, feeling sick, leaned forward and set the ends of her arms on the table. *Tanas.* The very name was venom to her mind. *So this is what he has been doing since we beat him last December.* He was playing the long game, she realized; he had been biding his time, watching from a distance, and plotting his revenge not only on the cookies who had betrayed him, but also on the mice who had aided them. His design was to destroy them all in one fell swoop, to wipe the Fur-Crumb Alliance from the map, and to exert his influence over both Cowtown and Sprinkleton. And if he succeeded in doing *that*, what then? Would he march to Mount Oniz with an army of voles and rogue cookies behind him? Would he reappear in his hometown and open a bakery called "Tanas's Tempting Treats" or something even worse? Ginger had no doubt that Mr. Theo could squash Tanas like a bug, but she bristled at the hubris. She was also angry that the man's tactics of trickery and seduction had continued; he had promised the voles the world—a world he would never actually give them once his demands were met—and they had accepted the bait gladly. They had conspired with their tempter, and as a result, Klaus and Ingrid and all the mice of Sweetfort would soon be marching their way to a massacre. The thought was far too horrible for such a scrumptious cookie like Ginger to consider.

"Bahar," said Molasses, "when I went astray last year, it was because I succumbed to my own evil desires. But it was Tanas who highlighted those desires and who convinced me that it would be worthwhile to betray my maker to fulfill them. He is the son of Mr. Theo and has spent years envious of his father. He's willing to do anything to mar his father's creatures."

Ginger nodded. "And if he can't mar them, he'll seek to remove them."

Bahar shook his head in apparent disbelief. "Then this news is all the graver for you, and for my vole allies."

"You have shared much, friend," said Agapa, "and at no small risk to yourself. May I ask why you parted with this information so willingly?"

"It has weighed heavily on my conscience—the starvation of the turkeys, the dastardly plan to have them devour the members of your alliance. But I was taught to trust in King Chisha's wisdom and to never doubt my vole brethren, so I've done my best to keep my head down and go on with my work. Then you showed up...and Ginger, you have told me how Klaus helped you last Christmas. Horace, you say that Klaus would never ask his followers to fight a battle he wouldn't fight himself. This is not the Klaus that I grew up hearing about. If what you say about him is true, I don't think it's fitting that he or his friends should perish in such an unjust fashion."

"Then you'll help us?" asked Ginger. "You'll help us stop Tanas from going through with his plan?"

"He has already begun." Bahar sighed. "The fool had this planned for months. He had a turkey run built; it's simply two long fences running parallel to each other, starting at his barn, going through the northern part of Lakeview Thicket, and ending near Great Boris's Stump."

Ginger looked at Agapa. "The wooden structures we saw earlier on the way here."

Agapa nodded at her. "He tells the truth."

"The turkeys can't fly over the boards," Bahar went on, "as they are too weak and the boards too tall. If everything is going according to schedule, Tanas has already opened the side door of his barn. The turkeys are making their way to the stump as we speak, and they should arrive well ahead of the scheduled 'duel.'"

"We need to leave!" cried Ginger. "We need to leave now!"

"It's almost two o'clock," replied Molasses. "To get to Great Boris's Stump in time, Klaus and the others will have already left. Knowing Klaus, he probably wanted to get there early to adjust to the terrain."

"You need to get to your friends quickly," said Bahar. "It's likely that the turkeys, spurred on by their liberation from the barn, will arrive at the stump faster than expected. We mice can hear well, but we can't outrun turkeys—not even weakened turkeys, because their hunger will drive them. The turkeys may see your friends before your friends hear them, and by then there will be no chance for escape."

"So we need to outpace the turkeys, somehow," said Ginger. "Can you help us with this, Bahar?"

"Maybe, and maybe not. There's a rumor floating around about a single turkey who has managed to avoid Tanas's barn. Despite many voles coming to him and trying to convince him that he will be protected from hunters by staying on Tanas's property, he has ignored every plea and fled from us—quite speedily, I might add. As the rumor goes, he refuses the offer not because he is wise; he is a conspiracy theorist and is always suspicious of ulterior motives. In this case, he has proven correct. He believed Tanas's generous offer to be a ruse, and so it was. But to his credit, despite his wackiness and distrust of absolutely *everyone* and *everything*, he has sought to free his brethren from the barn. He failed, though not for lack of trying; it's due rather to Tanas's extreme security measures, which could thwart even the most skilled impostor."

"Do you believe that this turkey would be altruistic enough to help us spare our friends?" asked Agapa.

"It's possible. After all, you would be proving his suspicions correct. You would be among the first to tell him that you believe his conspiracy theory to be true, and that might be enough to convince him to help you. No one is exempt from feeling the pride that comes with being told that one is right. If he agrees to join your cause, he could give you a ride on his back and outrun his emaciated kin."

Molasses looked closely at Bahar, studying him, as if trying to determine if *he* had an ulterior motive. "Can you take us to this turkey? Where is he?"

"Last I heard, he loiters right outside the barn of your great enemy. Do you think you're ready to be in the proximity of such great danger?"

Ginger looked at each of her friends in turn, and they gave her a single nod. She turned back to Bahar and did her best to emulate a shrug. "We have no choice, and we have no time to lose. But do you think you can afford to step away while your fellow guards wait for you? They didn't seem as eager to help us, or to give us the benefit of the doubt."

He turned from her and placed a paw against the wire mesh nearest him. "They'll either have to learn to wait or report me to the authorities. After months of striving to deny my guilt, I can't do so any longer. My conscience must be my authority." He turned his head toward the group. "We know our task, so let's get to it and get out of here before it's too late."

CHAPTER 4
Behind Enemy Lines

Their new vole ally, having warned them that retracing their steps through the attic was unsafe now that there was an awareness of their presence among the guards, let them out of the war room by unraveling a ball of thread and lowering them out a small hole in the attic vent. Bahar climbed down last of all and immediately led them behind an air conditioning unit, which concealed them from unwanted eyes; Ginger did not know what they were hiding from until she espied an old, furry dog roaming around on a lawn in what must have been the resident's back yard. The beast stood in place and sniffed the air a few times, but if he had smelled anything unusual, he did not show it; he stared blankly at nothing, panted, and then turned and walked the other way. They scurried across a strip of lawn to the north of the air conditioning unit and then made a left sharp turn and continued until they had reached a gate. Horace and Bahar combined their strength to push the bottom of the gate open just enough for the cookies to get through, then they squeezed their paunches through the small space and rejoined the group. The tall, untrimmed grass worked in their favor, hiding them from the drivers who raced down Cowtown's northernmost road.

As they waited for the traffic to pass, Ginger had some quiet time to think. She did not know how many days or years an enlivened gingerbread cookie would be granted on this earth, but she asked herself if she, her brother, and the rest of Mr. Theo's obedient creations would ever see the end of Tanas's schemes in their day. Sparing the land's turkeys to unleash them on his enemies was Tanas's latest plan, and she had already imagined what he might do if that plan succeeded; but what if he *failed*? Being one who had an abundance of resources and comrades, he could come up with a contingency plan, and another contingency plan, and another. She did not doubt that his devious strategies were without number. If the turkeys failed to do as he had commanded, maybe he would convince the voles to vanquish the Fur-Crumb Alliance (not that they needed too much convincing). And if *that* failed, then maybe he would use the Cookies of Tanas to infiltrate the Cookies of Theo and bring them down from the inside. It had already been proven that some of the *apparent* Cookies of Theo had never been his true followers at all, as they had left Mount Oniz and never returned. What if Tanas were to tell his followers to return to Theo and feign the seeking of forgiveness from and the reconciliation with those whom they had betrayed? Ginger grunted at the thought. Even if one of those cookies came to her and seemed sincere, she was not so sure she could forgive—not with ease, at least.

They had been hiding and waiting for about ten minutes when there was finally a lull in the traffic, and Bahar did not waste any time. He led them across the cold street and to the sidewalk on the other side, and in this place there were no houses—only a massive green field that extended into unknown northern lands. Just as they had made it over the sidewalk and tucked themselves behind a large rock, a car made a turn around the corner house in whose attic they had been loitering and drove past them. There were no cars immediately following, so they hurried away from the rock and breached the tall grass of the field. Here the earth was like a quagmire, muddy and sticky from recent rains, and filled with frogs nearly the size of Ginger. From what she had heard, amphibians generally did not care for sweets, but she was not going to get close enough to see if she had her facts straight.

Once they had gotten a fair distance from the road, Bahar made an announcement that it would take no more than fifteen minutes to reach Tanas's property, and that it would be wise for them to skirt the land along the south and east to reach the turkey fields on the far northern side of the region. They increased their speed as much as they were able, Agapa, Dave, and Reinhard using fishing line to tug them over the contrary terrain. Fifteen minutes' worth of travel seemed like a short distance, even for cookies who could only waddle fifty yards in a little under three minutes; but there was still the matter of convincing the turkey to run them back to Sprinklevale, followed by the monumental task of finding Klaus, the cookies, and the Mice of Sweetfort in an open field. Ginger struggled to ignore the fear gnawing at her, but she felt that they were already too far behind. If only she could relay the message to Klaus instantly—but they did not make phones or any kind of instant messaging devices for cookies and mice, and she was woefully reminded that she and her best friend had not yet mastered the art of telepathic communication.

Horace, despite his age and his reliance on his cane, did not seem bothered by the excessive mud. Several minutes into their journey through the grass, he began to stare at Bahar's back as if were suddenly entranced by the vole's sandpaper samurai armor. "This is mighty kind o' you, Bahar," he said at length, hopping over a twig. "In all muh years, I've only ever been told that the Voles of Cowtown were heathen brutes with nary an honorable bone in their bodies. I've heard your colonies have cursed Great Boris an' practiced witchcraft, that you've desecrated our temples, ambushed our kin, and demeaned us to our faces. It's refreshin' to see that you ain't all the same."

"I'm ashamed to admit that some of the stories you have heard are true," said Bahar. "Not that it's an excuse, but our animosity goes back decades, to the time of Great Boris. We were told that he looked down on us—that he would not give voles the time of day, and would not so much as entertain a weary vole sojourner. Though just from my interactions with you and hearing about Klaus, I'm beginning to guess that these stories were embellished. There are some more...decent voles in our midst, ones who may not be so different from you and your kin. But admittedly, there are many whose eyes are blind, and who still cling to the old ways without a second thought. Volsaph and Volahmi are among them. They hardly possess half a brain between them."

Ginger snickered. "Volahmi."

"Not now, Sister," Molasses said, but she could see a slight smirk on his face.

"And what of King Chisha?" asked Horace. "Is he half-brained or full-brained?"

"It would be best not to speak ill of my betters," replied Bahar, "but I'm not sure he has even one-fourth of a brain. He's rash, thoughtless, and despotic. He would sooner control those around them than listen to their needs. And he loves war more than he loves peace. The foremost thought in his mind is to expand his territory, and second to that is his desire to enact retribution on those who have wronged us. He's suspicious of everyone and would take no issue with slaying his own family members if they looked at him the wrong way."

"Sir Klaus is a very different kind of king," said Agapa. "Rashness and thoughtlessness have no place in him; he has ever been prudent and thoughtful. He listens carefully to those around him and weighs their advice, and this excursion is proof of that, for when Molasses declared that he suspected Volsaph to be hiding something, King Klaus commissioned us to investigate. He seeks the good and peace of the creatures around him and is quick to forgive. Those who are fortunate to be close to him, he loves and nurtures."

Reinhard pranced animatedly. "The cookies of Mount Oniz still recite the story of Klaus the Brave crossing the vale to exchange his life for Horace, Arthur, and Ingrid when they were taken by King Shol!"

"I know of Ingrid, the queen," said Bahar, "but I have not heard of this *Arthur*. Who is he?"

Horace bowed his head. "He was a bear of a mouse with a big ol' heart. I loved 'im like a brother, and so did King Klaus and Queen Ingrid. Arthur fought against the enemies of Ginger and Klaus sev'al months ago but fell in battle. He gave up his life right willing, he did, and with his last breath, told Klaus that he needed to step into kingship and unite the mice of the vale."

"Then Arthur fully trusted Klaus to be worthy of the kingship," said Bahar, "and it was so important to him that he spent his final moments speaking of it. He must have truly believed in Klaus."

"Oh, he did. We all did, and do."

"It's a shame I've never met the mouse for myself—Klaus, that is."

"It is not too late, Bahar," Agapa told him, smiling.

A curious gleam came to the vole's eye. "Perhaps not."

The earth gradually hardened and began to descend with steady increments. Ginger found that travel became easier at this juncture, almost effortless, and her mood improved with every step. Until this point, she had felt that they had been "swimming upstream," as the saying went: migrating to another town under a time constraint, attempting to sneak through an attic without being spotted, waiting for traffic to pass, and wriggling through a veritable bog just to reach their destination. Now she observed how their pace had quickened, how the grass scintillated under the muted autumn sun, and how the birds winged their way through the sky and trilled their cheery tunes. For the first time today, a broad smile stretched across her face and remained there. A burden lifted from where her shoulders might have been, and she breathed a loud sigh of relief and proceeded to walk carefree. Molasses did the same, it appeared; his arms no longer twitched for his whisk, and his body was straight and his face beaming. It was nice that they could let their guards down for once. Reinhard walked between them, glancing back and forth at the pair but remaining silent.

A few minutes later they came to a lip of land overlooking a sharper decline, and that was when Ginger beheld a building—or more accurately, a mansion, single-story but thrice the length and width of the average house, coated with beautiful white paint and high, steeple-like eaves. There was an inviting aura around it, a promise of hospitality for weary travelers. Ginger was reminded of Mr. Theo's house—the wood paneling and arced windows were almost exact copies—but this building had a different appeal that she could not quite put her metaphorical finger on. A broad porch with visibly comfy chairs stretched across the entirety of the front of the home, and a white, brick walkway wended between grey rocks until it came to the place where the travelers' slope ended. Over to the left was an immense fenced-in field, wherein countless crops and fruit-bearing trees grew. Every acre of the property was invariably pleasing to the eye.

Ginger knew better than to be tempted by such obvious seduction; in fact, she almost let out a laugh at Tanas's ploy. She did not need any of his dangling dainties or his captivating comforts. She liked to think that her experiences over the past eleven months had grown her at an accelerated rate, and that the temptations of the past were less attractive than they had once been. Tanas could stuff his empty promises; she had no need to linger near his habitation. No, Ginger would not be so easily enticed—not again. She would help her friends speak to the turkey and save the Fur-Crumb Alliance. Then they would all return to Klaus's place and enjoy the time together that they had planned.

You shouldn't even be out here in the first place, she grumbled internally. *You should be finishing up the last bit of decorating at your friend's house and enjoying pleasant conversation with Klaus and Ingrid. You should be sitting around a warm fire, listening to Agapa and Reinhard lift their voices in song. You should be giggling as Dave regales the group with stories of couples whom he has recently caused to fall in love with his arrows. We cookies should be looking forward to the close of this month, when the people of Sprinkleton begin setting out their Christmas decorations. Should, should, should. But we're not doing any of those things. We're out in the wild, cleaning up another mess made by Tanas, with the lives of our loved ones hanging in the balance. Nothing is going according to plan. It's all ruined.*

She glared long at Tanas's house and felt her smile turn into a frown. *It's all his fault that this day has been ruined. It's his fault that I'm not getting my way. It's his fault that King Chisha's mice were led astray by his produce. It's his fault that Volsaph marched his way into Sweetfort and challenged Klaus to a duel. It's his fault that we have had to trudge through mud to speak to a turkey who probably won't even help us. In fact, I wouldn't be surprised to know that we're too late already. Maybe Klaus and the Alliance reached Great Boris's Stump early, and the turkeys rushed over there, and all our friends are dead. Maybe this has been a fool's errand, and we would have been better suited to flee from Sprinklevale altogether. Why did Molasses suggest we come all the way out here? If he suspected a trap, why didn't he have us run the other direction?* Her internal groaning became audible, and the relaxed feeling that had settled upon her just minutes earlier dissipated altogether. Suddenly, she felt so very *tired*, and irritable, and frustrated. *I've had enough.*

"Ginger?" Bahar said, looking back at her. "Is something the matter?"

She shook herself free of her thoughts. "Oh, no, not really. I just—I think there's something I need to do, while we're in the area. A quick detour. Would it be okay if I caught up with you in a few minutes?"

Her companions gave her a blank stare, but then Molasses waved an arm and said, "Don't worry, friends. I'll go with her. I think I know what's on her mind."

"Don't tarry long," Bahar warned them. "You must leave Cowtown within the hour if you wish to reach your friends in time."

"We'll be back before you know it," replied Ginger. "Pinky promise."

She and Molasses left the group behind, and she heard them discussing the nature of a pinky promise and how binding it was on a legal scale, as well as whether a cookie with no fingers could be held to such a solemn vow. But soon she heard not a single voice, for the whistle of the wind and her own thoughts drowned out every competing sound.

Within a couple of minutes, she and her brother had reached the fence bordering Tanas's ranch. The radiant house faced south, but a red and white barn, surrounded by a corral containing goats, faced east. This was where the wicked son of Mr. Theo had kept the unsuspecting rafter of turkeys, and where the poor beasts had suffered extreme hunger for weeks. She could see a door standing ajar on the barn's left side and the beginning of the turkey run leading west across the field and into Lakeview Thicket. As for the house itself, warm, beckoning light pulsed against the windows, vainly pledging a soul's respite for all those willing to turn aside and enter. Ginger had been staring at one of these windows for a few seconds when a figure stepped into the light and peered out at the land; or perhaps the figure was peering out at her and Molasses. She did not need to be told who stood there, nor did she need a closer look. Tanas, that great deceiver, was waiting for someone to tempt, waiting for someone to devour.

"There's the devil," Molasses muttered. "I loathe him for who he is and what he's done to Mr. Theo's creation. His antics have even affected the mice of the land, who have nothing to do with our struggles. He should have left them out of it."

"I think they became a part of it even before the Fur-Crumb Alliance existed, Brother," Ginger told him with shame. "The moment I enlisted Klaus's aid the night of Christmas Eve, I brought them into this."

"Still, you were just protecting the vale. And it seems he has taken Klaus's help personally."

"Do you really think he believed he could wipe us all out in one fell swoop?" She scowled at the thought. "Is he that arrogant?"

"He is *definitely* that arrogant. But he's also wily. If he were to fail killing *all* of us, he could do even more damage by making the surviving Cookies of Theo face despair over the loss of their loved ones. Despair can be paralyzing, and it can ignite both new trespasses and old."

"Don't I know it...." She released a sigh and swept the end of her right leg through the dirt. "So we're here, a stone's throw from the one who has made our lives miserable. What do we do?"

He took his whisk from his back and swung it once through the air. "We finish this, once and for all."

How? the wiser part of herself wanted to ask; but instead, she replayed the evil deeds that Tanas had enacted upon her and others ever since her inception. She did not think Molasses would get very far by bashing a man's bare leg with pure cookie-strength, but at the very least, they could give him a piece of their minds. "He needs to be stopped," she acceded, "but do you think we're ready for him?"

The corners of his mouth had fallen in sadness and rage. She knew how personal this was for him. "How long are we going to let him get away with this? How long are we going to let others pay for what we have done?"

"I understand, I do. I just—" She took a big breath and bowed her head. "No, Brother, you're right. We're responsible for the sickening rosemary scent that plagues us cookies and the fallout that has affected the Alliance, but it was all instigated by him. If you think we can do something about it, then I trust you. So...lead the way! But just be careful, okay? I don't think he'll welcome his betrayer with open arms."

"He might, if he thinks he can win me back." Molasses shook his head to relay the message that the event was an impossibility. "Let's go."

They went, breaching the property by ducking beneath a space in the fence. Perhaps Ginger was just imagining it, but something changed the moment she touched the soil of that land. The produce, which had seemed detestable to her at a distance, shone with splendorous color now that they were closer. The plumpness of the fruits and vegetables was undeniable, and she wondered what Tanas had used for soil, or how he could possibly afford to water his crops and trees to their current level of healthiness, or why his produce looked superior to varieties she had seen elsewhere. She was incapable of consuming such comestibles, but she could still *look*, if she wished, and there was no harm in *looking*, of course. She also noticed that beneath some of the trees were spacious places with verdant grass and small pools of water, miniature paradises that appeared perfect for someone of her size.

How brilliantly the cold autumn sunlight gleamed against the dew-flecked leaves of a plant that twisted itself around a trellis! How magnificent and deeply hued were the flowers that opened themselves to the light of day! They *spoke* to her, she was quite certain, imploring her to turn aside and refresh herself. What was an extra minute or two, anyway, when she and her friends had been away from Sprinkleton for half a day? Would she not be of far more use to her friends if she returned to them revitalized? Yes, they would *prefer her* to be revitalized. A bit of quiet solitude would do her good.

She meandered to the left and half-noticed that Molasses was doing the same, his whisk now having returned to his back. They were heading toward a rosebush, dark and healthy and blooming, its red flowers as wide as small plates; beneath it stretched a pavilion of grass, light green as unripe lime from regular watering. "Come, sit, rest," said the roses. "Regain your strength. Here you shall be renewed, if only you soak yourself in the ease and comfort of this place. Shrug aside your burden; there is no need to be watchful, nor must you be on guard. The struggle is out there, in the world, but there is no struggle *here*. So come and stay. Sit, rest."

Ginger and Molasses heeded the voice. They came to the rosebush and were enamored by its red flowers, and feeling a sense of restfulness, they sat in the shade of that bush, thinking that the shade would assist them in recovering from their weariness. However, the shade receded with almost imperceptible movements, forcing the two cookies to inch closer and closer to the bush. Over the course of several minutes, they scooted ever closer to the thick vines, scarcely aware that large thorns threatened to tear into their crumbly exteriors. It was Ginger who noticed that a shadow thrown by a large flower was receding slower than the other shadows, so she asked Molasses to join her and, looking down at the delightful grass, they lethargically moved over to it. By the time they lifted their heads, they were shocked to see the thorns right before them—and it appeared that the plant was leaning forward to harm them!

"Help, Brother!" cried Ginger. "I was deceived again! And now...I don't know what to do. Please, help me get out of this!"

"I'm sorry, Sister, but I can't help you!" said Molasses, who stood beside her in a state of paralysis. "I'm about to be struck, myself! I can't—I can't pull myself away!"

"What do we do?"

"I don't know. I didn't prepare for this." He looked here and there, wild-eyed. "Help! Someone, please help! Mr. Theo!"

Yes, Mr. Theo. "Mr. Theo, help!" Ginger called out. "Please!"

Something, or someone, told her that it was no use calling out—that Mr. Theo had ignored her for months in that prison, and that he would not listen to her now. This temptation she was able to resist, for she remembered her miraculous escape, and how her maker had used that time in prison to grow her. He *had* heard her back then, and he could hear her now.

"Mr. Theo!" she shouted all the louder. "We've followed our own wills and gone after our own desires again. Please help!"

For some reason, there was a prompting within that she should look to her left, and sensing that this prompting was good and right, she obeyed it. That's when she realized there was a voice coming from that direction.

"If any of you believes in me, though you are split asunder in this life, you have no need to fear the Scariest Place," said the voice. "The Scariest Place is one of darkness and hopelessness, and there are some who have already tasted of it. That need not be true for those who hear me now."

Ginger turned her head further to the left, and there she saw a shortbread cookie in the shape of a lamb standing on top of a fence before a crowd of listeners. Among them were Clove, Limerence, and Frostina, who were at the front of the audience; behind them stood a Christmas tree cookie, a snowman cookie, a handsome hat-donning gingerbread man and a purple-bowed gingerbread woman, and several Cupid cookies. Ginger recognized some among the latter group cookies, for they had been present during the Christmas Eve battle and had fled after their defeat at the paws of the Colony Behind the Cabinets. In the back, sulking and watching from a distance, was Eggy the miniature gingerbread cookie. It was Eggy who, around Independence Day, had aided Frostina in torturing Limerence and in breaking his wings. She had fought for the Cookies of Theo in the skirmish that followed Ginger's liberation from prison but had snuck away in the aftermath without a word to anyone, presumably ashamed of bringing harm to a fellow cookie at Frostina's behest. Ginger wondered where Eggy stood now in her allegiance. Perhaps it was promising that she was separate from the rest of the Cookies of Tanas, listening not with defiance (for many of the other cookies scowled at the lamb), but with humility and hope.

"Who do you think you are?" Frostina demanded, shifting her body closer to the fence. "What makes you think you have any greater authority than we do? Weren't you created after the rest of us?"

"Before any of you jumped off the pan, I already existed," answered the lamb cookie. "I was there with Mr. Theo, in his kitchen, at the beginning. You came long after."

Clove shook his head and looked at Frostina. "This maniac thinks he's better than the rest of us."

"Mr. Theo has provided the way for all cookies to be in good standing with him once again," the shortbread cookie continued. "You have been cut off from his kitchen, but today he has shown you the way back to him."

"What...way?" Limerence asked, sounding timider than he had the last time Ginger had heard him speak. "What are you talking about?"

"*I* am the way to him," was the lamb's answer, "and I am the *only* way. So turn from your wicked ways and come while there is yet time. Mr. Theo stands ready to forgive, even if your evil deeds are as high as heaven. You must trust in the one who made you, and trust in his lamb, who will taste death so that Mr. Theo's chosen cookies need never suffer its sting.

"Some here may have heard of Ethad, the great fish from Lake Sysba, who hungers for cookies and promises them death. And beyond him lies the Scariest Place, destined for those who finally reject Mr. Theo and his lamb cookie. Those who forsake their evil way and come to me should not fear Ethad or the Scariest Place. Mr. Theo will forgive, and he will forgive to the uttermost."

And what about those who have already trusted Mr. Theo and still struggle? Ginger wondered, feeling something akin to heartbreak within. *Is it too late for us?*

Perhaps she was imagining it, but she thought that the lamb cookie had raised his head to look at her. "Mr. Theo's chosen—those who love him and who heed his voice—must stand ready to forgive those who have wronged them. Even if their fellow cookie wrongs them four hundred ninety times and comes to them asking for forgiveness, they must no longer count the trespasser's misdeeds against him. For so does Mr. Theo forgive his dear ones."

Four hundred ninety times? Ginger's mind could not comprehend it. *That number seems pretty random, but...is Mr. Theo's mercy truly that great?*

It is even greater, she thought she heard a voice say. *Now leave your trespasses at my feet and continue on your way, for there is much that you must yet undertake for the sake of the one who loves you.*

Molasses must have received the same message, for just as she wrested herself from her daze and took a step forward, her brother did likewise. Ginger noticed that the lamb was now gazing out at the crowd once more and beginning a treatise on his identity. But Ginger knew his identity; he spoke with the voice of Mr. Theo, and his words *were* Mr. Theo's. Her maker was still baking on Mount Oniz, already starting on his Christmas cookies for the month to come; but somehow he was also *here*, in the province of the enemy, with her and with her brother. Tanas seemed to know the lamb's identity, too, because when she looked over at his house, she realized that he had closed all his blinds and apparently retreated farther into the building. The moment she saw that he was gone, she and her brother took a breath and felt the weight of the temptation fade. Behind them, the thorny rosebush retracted, having failed to fully entangle them. They smiled at each other and turned away, aiming for the nearest path that would take them away from Tanas's property.

CHAPTER 5
Trot

A few minutes later, they came to the field north of the man's ranch and spotted their friends. Bahar and Agapa stood on the precipice of a ridge of land just beyond the northernmost fence, gazing into the blur of green that lay ahead; the grass near the precipice was freshly trimmed (probably by Tanas, who had never really seemed to understand boundaries, anyway), so the cookies and mice were hard to miss. Dave and Horace were engaged in quiet conversation when Ginger and Molasses reached them.

"Glad to see the detour was quick as you said," Horace muttered, waving his cane in the air. "With the lives of our kin on the line, we need all paws an' crumbs on deck."

"Did you do what you needed to do?" asked Dave.

Ginger shared a glance with her brother. "Yes, we did," they said in unison.

"And did you learn what you needed to learn?" Agapa asked them. She gave them a knowing look, a look that relayed an entire message: *It was foolish of you to think you could confront Tanas in your own strength. He is far more powerful than we are. None of us is exempt from succumbing to his temptations, or to the temptations of his minions. Only Mr. Theo can overcome him.*

"Yes," Molasses chimed in, "we learned so great a lesson, it was as if we had sat at the feet of our maker himself and heard him speak directly to us."

"Good," Agapa said, her eyes brightening.

"It *is* good," agreed Bahar, "and now we can continue with our important task." He gestured with his head, and Ginger saw that he had already discovered the turkey's location. The feathered beast was huge, about the size of what she had always imagined something like a bear cub to be. Its feathers were a rich dark brown, almost black, and appeared waxy in the afternoon sunlight; some of them were jutting out in random directions, not uniform with the others. Its tail was like a folding fan and broader than the rest of its body. Beneath its plunging beak was its wattle, crimson and saggy, and it vibrated every time the creature gobbled—which was quite often. Now and then it would open its wings and scrape the ground with its sharp talons. Ginger did not know much about turkeys, but she was immediately worried that this one was as feral as they came and that it would have no qualms about eating her in one big, beaky bite.

"*That's* what you're hanging your hope on?" Molasses asked Bahar, poking him with the end of his arm. "*That* thing?"

"He *looks* dangerous," Bahar answered, "and frankly, he probably *is* dangerous in some ways. And I won't lie: he is insane. Purely out of his mind. How do the humans put it? He has *lost his marbles*, if he had any marbles to begin with. But he was right about Tanas's deceit, and from what I've heard, he has a code of honor. I doubt that he wants his friends to do the bidding of their captor and eat the enemies of his enemies."

"So how do we approach him?" asked Dave. "Do we surround him so he has nowhere to run?"

"That might spook him; he might feel cornered, or as though he is about to be attacked. I think it would be best if we approached him in small groups, one group at a time, over the course of a few minutes."

"Then we best get going now," said Horace, stretching. "Time's a-wastin'."

It was decided that Agapa and Dave should fly out first, for there was something majestic and lovable about their appearance (or that is the way Bahar put it, at least, to Ginger's chagrin and mild jealousy), and they might succeed at putting the turkey at ease before the others joined the group. The Cupid cookies fluttered out over the field and met with the turkey not fifty yards from the ridge where the others waited. From what Ginger could see, the feathered beast did not appear to be startled or more suspicious than expected, and already she could hear him speaking with openness and delight. Once or twice she thought she heard him laugh, an astonishing development considering that Agapa and Dave were not all that funny. After a couple of minutes, the Cupid cookies waved toward the ridge, and she and her brother headed across the field.

"These are our friends, Ginger and Molasses," Agapa explained to the turkey. "They are Cookies of Theo, also, coming from Mount Oniz."

"Well, Mount Oniz is the highest mountain in California, you know!" the bird squawked. "That's what they say on the grapevine, at least. Why do they call it the grapevine?" He stared at Ginger and Molasses for a good ten seconds, as though he expected them to answer. When they did not, he let out a great gobble of a laugh. "I'm just pulling your surely delectable legs. I'm Trot! Put 'er there!"

Molasses's face scrunched with thought. "Put her where? And who is 'her'?"

"That's just what we turkeys say when we meet new turkeys. We say it, then we bash our wings together." He displayed his left wing to demonstrate. "But you don't have wings, far as I can see. Not like Agapa and Dave here."

Ginger placed the ends of her arms where her hips might have been. "You seem to be in pretty good spirits, considering everything that's going on."

"You mean Thanksgiving?" He looked at Molasses. "Does she mean Thanksgiving?" He then looked at no one in particular. "She must mean Thanksgiving. Yea, surely do I weep for my brethren who will be feasted on this evening. Theirs was a necessary sacrifice to keep the humans content. Without human contentment, the land would not be so primed for turkey contentment. Although there are *some* turkeys whom I will not name—such as myself—who claim we would fare just fine without human intervention. I suspect—" He stopped, his beady eyes glazing over. "No, no, I've said too much already. Ears everywhere."

"She speaks not of Thanksgiving," said Agapa, "but of the impending doom that may yet befall King Klaus and the members of the Fur-Crumb Alliance. The turkeys whom Tanas has held captive for weeks have been loosed from his barn, and to our knowledge, they presently make for Sprinklevale by way of yonder pathway."

"Is that what the scoundrel did?" Trot's feathers bristled. "I knew he was up to something. I told my buddy, Tom, that I believed Tanas to be in cahoots with extraterrestrials, but I guess he doesn't need outside influence for his evil designs."

"He doesn't," Molasses said. "Now, because of his plan, we fear for the lives of our friends. The Mice of Sweetfort and Cookies of Theo, who follow King Klaus, have been duped by the Voles of Cowtown into meeting at a stump just west of here. The voles will not be there to meet them, but your fellow turkeys *will*...."

"And will eat every last one of them," Trot deducted with a nod. "And there's an alliance, you say, between King Klaus and your fellow cookies? Yeah, my friends will eat them too. And why wouldn't they? They are *hungry*. I think they would eat a small child if given the chance. Kidding!" He lowered his head and looked here and there. "Totally kidding."

"We need your help, Trot," Ginger told him, stepping forward. "Please."

"Well, you *sound* sincere. And I simply *adore* that bow you're wearing. Look at the tiny turkeys standing next to the tiny pumpkins! They're turkeys! They're tiny! I love them!" He chuckled as though he had heard the funniest joke in the world, then became deadly serious and narrowed his eyes. "Let's say I believe you. Maybe I do, maybe I don't. That depends on the source of your information."

Agapa waved at Bahar, Horace, and Reinhard, and the trio scurried across the grass. Bahar managed to offer an extravagant flourish despite his armor, and Horace, clearly less certain about relying on a turkey for help, tucked his cane under his belly and bowed his head. Reinhard moved his head to the left and to the right as a way to extend a respectful greeting.

After the three had offered their names by way of introduction, Trot studied them for almost half a minute before snorting and saying, "That there's a vole."

"Trot, trust us, this one is different," Dave insisted. "He told us of Tanas's plot and risked his neck by sneaking us out of the house where King Chisha's kingdom stands. We had been spying and were caught, but Bahar led us out and—well, he led us to you."

"What do you have to gain from telling these cookies and this practically ancient mouse about Tanas's plot?" Trot inquired, bringing his head almost eye level to Bahar. "Huh? Riddle me that, Bilhur!"

Bahar's body slumped as he sighed. "Death, more than likely."

"Death?"

"Yes." The vole turned his eyes to the bright grass curling between his paws. "I have served King Chisha since the day I was born. I have always thought highly of him and never imagined my allegiance being placed anywhere else. But seeing how he entrusted himself to one like Tanas, whose evil deeds speak for themselves, I lost respect for my king and for those who follow him blindly. Tanas starved innocent creatures, and King Chisha helped him get away with it, never raising his voice in opposition. I might have remained quiet and tried to ignore the warnings in my mind, but then these fine cookies and this dutiful mouse showed up in my home. If they are a sample of the kinds of mice and cookies to be found in the Fur-Crumb Alliance, and if King Klaus is as selfless as they claim him to be, then I can't do as my kin have done. I can't let Tanas's dastardly plan unfold. If my friends here mean to stop him, then I will do what I can to make sure their mission succeeds."

Trot's eyes grew large. "Wow. That was something, wasn't it?" He shook his head and attempted to whistle but, having no lips, failed miserably. "Brilliant, brilliant speech. Reminds me of a young Tap-a-Tap, this one. Yeah, in all but appearance." He allowed a moment's silence to hang in the air. "No one knows Tap-a-Tap? The famous turkey orator? What, do you all live under rocks?"

"We live under a storm drain," replied Horace.

"Garage," said Bahar.

"We have no excuse," said Ginger, gesturing toward her fellow cookies. "We're just ignorant."

"And honest, it seems!" Trot responded with a laugh. "Fine, fine. So you cookies are allied with King Klaus. This geezer here, Horse or whatever you call him, must be one of King Klaus's advisors; he looks like the mice who roam those parts, at least. You suspected Tanas was up to something, so you came all the way over here and were briefed by Bilhan. Now you're trying to stop my friends from eating all of *your* friends. Is that right?"

"Except for a few mispronunciations of names, yes," said Molasses.

Trot's beak puckered as he considered each member of the group in turn. He hummed to himself and began to walk here and there, sometimes facing Lakeview Thicket to the west, sometimes gazing at the foothills to the northeast, and sometimes turning again to his guests. He stretched out his wings and flapped them once, twice, thrice—and Ginger wondered if they had wasted their time by requesting aid from the most indecisive bird in a fifty-mile radius. She looked up at the sun and frowned as she saw how late in the day it had grown. *We need to get back to the vale*, she thought. *We can't afford to be here any longer.*

As if reading her mind, Trot abruptly hopped in the group's direction and narrowed his gaze at her. "You seem to be the spokeswoman of this band of misfits, oh beautifully-dressed one. Why did you come to me. I mean...why me?"

She adjusted her bow with pride at the sound of the compliment and then pressed the ends of her arms together. "Trot, if what Bahar says is true, then all the turkeys of the land have become victimized by Tanas. They all fell for his plan—all of them except you. Surely, you don't want your friends to further the purposes of that evil man, and we don't want our friends to die. We need to get back to Sprinklevale quickly, but...well, have you seen our legs?"

Trot nodded vigorously. "Scrumptious. Puny."

"Exactly. And with such scrumptious and puny legs, we can't exactly hoof it back home in time to warn our friends, nor can we drive. They don't make cars for cookies."

"Not yet, at least," said Trot, "but new inventions are springing up every day."

"I think we can help each other," Ginger continued. "Give us a ride to Sprinklevale and help us save our friends, and you'll keep *your* friends from committing a great evil at the hands of Tanas."

The turkey lanced his talons through the grass and let out a long sigh. "You know, I tried to warn them. It just seemed too convenient; this man builds a farm a stone's throw from where we roam, and a month out from Thanksgiving, he offers to open up his barn and protect my friends from hunters? What did *he* get out of that? It seemed too good to be true, and clearly it was. One by one he led them through those gates, even as I screamed my protests from the other side of the fence. But I can understand why they accepted the offer. Dozens of us are killed around this time every year and made the centerpiece of every human family's table. Many of our loved ones are lost...but at least in that situation we are actually doing some good; the humans are sustained, so someone is benefiting. All that my friends have done in Tanas's barn is wasted away, groaning in their malnourishment—and for what? So he could sit back and twiddle his thumbs while he waited for the right time to unleash them on his enemies? He made them pawns. They had no purpose of their own. And now, driven by their hunger, they have no choice but to do whatever he says.

"Those turkeys should be free, celebrating Thanksgiving. On this day each year, we congregate in the forest and gobble our songs of thanks, and we lift up our gratitude to the One who made the earth, who sustains it, and who gives us daily provision. That day was stolen from my kin by a selfish man. I had resigned in helping them see reason, but maybe if I have you with me, we can convince them together."

Ginger almost jumped with joy. "Does that mean you'll help us?"

"As long as you swear to me that you're not working with extraterrestrials, then yes, I'll help you."

"We're not working with extraterrestrials," she replied, "but even if we were, do you think we would tell you?"

"That's a great answer. You're wise beyond your years, Mrs. Cookie."

"That's 'Ms. Cookie.' I'm not married."

Trot tilted his head to the side. "You're not? Well, never say never."

"I didn't."

"Another great answer. I marvel at your intellectual prowess, Ginger." He turned to the rest of the group and extended his wings. "Tanas released my friends into the turkey run about an hour ago. I'm sure they're making their way to Sprinklevale as fast as they can, but as I said before, they're weakened by their hunger. They may have to stop to rest from time to time, or they may slow to a walk to recover their strength. If we're going to pass them and warn your friends in time, we should leave now. We can discuss specifics as to where I'm running along the way."

"How, er, do you advise we do this?" asked Horace. "I mean, how're you going to carry all seven of us?'

"You mice and the gingerbread cookies will have to hang on to my feathers for dear life. I'll move faster than a rushing river, and I don't stop for anyone, so if you fall off, you're done. End of story." He tittered and swept one wing through the air. "Kidding! I'll go back for you if the mood hits me." He gestured toward Agapa, Dave, and Reinhard. "Cupid cookies! Small deer! Looks like you have conveniently brought some fishing line with you. There aren't any fish around here, not for a mile or so! But you could tie some fishing line around my neck and hold on as I pull you through the air."

Molasses clapped once. "Then it sounds like that's all settled. I guess there's just one last thing to confirm." He turned to the armored vole who stood beside him. "Bahar, you've come all this way, and we're eternally grateful for all that you've done and all that you've risked. But what will you do now? Will you see this through to the end? Will you come with us?"

Bahar tapped the square of armor that protected his left thigh, and his tail flicked through the grass as if it had a mind of its own. He bowed his head. "I'm afraid I can't leave just yet. Trot seeks to save his friends from obeying Tanas's orders. You seek to rescue your friends from ravenous turkeys. And what of *my* friends? What of those who have, until now, been too blind to see how far King Chisha and we voles have gone astray? I must try to awaken them; I must help them see that there's a better way. If even one listens to me, it would mean the world." He stepped forward and came to Ginger and Molasses, and then his voice dropped to a whisper so that only they could hear him. "Travel with Trot, but take care to avoid the section of the forest directly northeast of Great Boris's Stump. Volsaph and half of our kingdom is there, hoping to watch the decimation of the Fur-Crumb Alliance. You must approach from southeast of the stump to avoid detection." He gave them a stern look. "I've just shared the location of many of my kind. They are villains, sold out for Tanas. Do what you will with that information."

"Best of luck, Barham," said Trot, saluting him with one wing. The bird was already stretching his legs and rolling his head in circles in preparation for his mad dash to Sprinklevale.

"Safe travels, Trot. And all of you." Bahar nodded to them and turned toward Cowtown. He stepped in that direction, but then he hesitated and turned back around. "If you proved successful in your mission, and I were to find my way to you at some point—"

"You would be welcomed with open arms," answered Molasses, "and we would see you as one of our own."

Tears came to Bahar's eyes. "How wonderful. How wonderful, indeed." Then he left them and raced off into the southern horizon.

CHAPTER 6
The Race to Sprinklevale

The speed that Trot employed in his race through Lakeview Thicket was unlike anything that Ginger had ever experienced. At first she held onto his neck, which felt as strong and secure as a pillar; but very quickly she realized that the wind blew with greater force up front, and she found herself holding on with both arms while her legs trailed behind her. She eventually tucked herself in the space between Trot's left wing and his body, poking her head out on occasion to determine where they were and to shout out directions. Molasses was there beside her, one arm clutching the nearest feather and the other around her—though whether that was for her own protection or because he was just being a big fat scaredy cat, she did not know. Horace, nestled under the turkey's right wing, seemed to be having the time of his life; he raised his front paws high in the air with many a whoop and cheer, his whiskers flailing back around his head in the wind's wake. Agapa and Dave had learned that it was better to refrain from flapping their wings and simply glide through the air, as any wing movement created drag and impeded their momentum. They and Reinhard were soaring many feet behind, fishing line wrapped around their bodies.

"We're too far north, Trot!" yelled Ginger. "We need to start turning south."

"The fastest way between two points, assuming you're not an extraterrestrial and haven't been blessed with the ability to teleport, is a straight line!" the bird replied. "Why go south?"

"Just—trust me. We approach from the south and then turn north, a little west of Great Boris's Stump. I'm hoping we can cut off Klaus and the others while they're still on their way."

"Fine. I'll trust in your waferly wisdom, Big-Brain. Wait, do you have a brain?"

"No, no internal organs. I don't have a brain, but I do have a mind."

"That makes no sense!" The turkey paused as if to think about it more carefully. "Nope, that really makes no sense at all! But south we go, Ms. Cookie!"

Until that point, Trot had been dashing abreast of the turkey run as much as possible, and there had been no sign of his friends. Now, as he veered around a boulder and began a southwestern trajectory, Ginger gazed to the right across the top of his body and spotted the last in the line of turkeys. They were gobbling so loudly that the sound reverberated across every tree, and although Ginger had only met her first turkey minutes earlier, she thought she was picking up a tone of deep distress in their gobbles. *Their situation is more desperate than we knew*, she mused. *They're truly starving and are not in their right minds. Anything that crosses their path, anything that can serve as food, they'll tear to pieces. Maybe even me.*

So fast did they move through the forest that it was nothing more than a blur of olive green and bark brown and stone grey in her vision. Trot dodged between trees, leapt over rocks and shrubs, and splashed without slowing through babbling brooks. The canopy of pine needles overhead danced between patches of cloudy sky in a confusing tangle of color. Even the sounds of animals in the region—the deer, woodpeckers, and peacocks—commingled in a song that seemed to urge the turkey to reach his destination with all possible haste. Ginger decided that this was the fastest she ever wanted to move; the humans could have their cars, their roller coasters, and their other innumerable speedy contraptions.

The turkey run was almost out of sight when they crashed out into the field of Sprinklevale, but it was obvious that the creatures had not yet left the forest, as their gobbles were no longer audible. Within another minute or so, Ginger could see the outline of Great Boris's Stump to the north. Trot must have also seen it, for he made a gradual northwestern turn toward Mount Oniz—toward her home. Mr. Theo was up there, she knew, having closed up shop early because of the holiday. He was in his kitchen, consulting a list he had established long ago, and considering possible modifications to the icing he would use for his next batch of cookies, or ruminating on types of baked goods other than gingerbread, trees, and snowmen that he could provide to the townspeople. He had baked some pastries and crackers for Halloween and Thanksgiving, but none had sprung to life. This did not mean that the man's creative power had somehow waned; Ginger suspected that more cookies would receive souls in the future, some pledging allegiance to their maker and others to the one who sought to dethrone him. She tried not to think much about a fresh batch of enemies, and instead pondered what manner of new and unexpected friends she might have, and how they might help in the fight against Tanas.

It was inevitable for her to wonder why Mr. Theo did not seem to be taking a more active role in thwarting the deeds of his wayward son. Everyone knew that he was wiser and stronger, but for reasons that may have been known only to him and to the lamb cookie, he was *waiting*, not *acting*. He baked as he had always baked; he provided as he had always provided; he loved as he had always loved. But when it came to the one who had rebelled against him, he was delaying judgment. Why was he doing this? Why was he allowing his enemy to get a foothold in certain areas and exist as a constant threat to the cookies whom he cared for? *Maybe he is* actively *waiting*, thought Ginger. *Maybe Tanas's defeat is so certain that it is practically a done deal to Mr. Theo. But in the meantime, maybe he means to grow us cookies through the challenges, through the temptations, through the times when the enemy puts a hitch in our plans. And it's not as if we're without a promise. How did he put in his letter to us? "I, your father of peace, will soon crush Tanas beneath your feet." How long must we wait before we see that happen?*

Molasses peeked out from Trot's feathers and extended an arm in the direction of the distant stump. "It looks like Volsaph and the other voles are nowhere to be seen. Bahar's intel was accurate!"

"Klaus and the others aren't there, either, thankfully!" Ginger responded. "We still have a chance to cut them off!"

"When you two are done shouting back there, any way you could give a poor old bird some directions?" asked Trot, glancing back at them. "Are we just going to keep going until we reach the mountain, or—"

"Okay, start moving north in a straight line, then turn west once the stump is directly to your right."

"Got it! Alright, hang on, my bite-sized friends!"

He shifted gently to the right, and a few seconds later he made a sharp turn left toward the fields north of Sprinkleton. The grass glittered with fresh rain, and Ginger was surprised how one area could experience such a shower while an area just a mile away could remain cloudy and dry. The cold wind tickled her, shifting larger and darker clouds into the sky overhead and threatening a downpour. She hoped that they managed to save the day and conclude this adventure in short order, not only for the sake of her loved ones, but also because she just *detested* walking around as a soggy mess. Cookies and rain would never mix.

She scanned the territory ahead of them for any sign of the Mice of Sweetfort, but she saw nothing more than a few frogs, squiggly worms, and some freakishly colossal snails. The vastness of Sprinklevale, at least for a cookie, became acutely obvious to her; the fields between the town and Mount Oniz could take days for a cookie to fully sweep, and even then, if proper care were not taken, patches of field could be missed. What if they were to run to the other side of the vale and somehow bypass Klaus completely, and the mice and cookies reached the stump in the meantime? *Or what if they never left Sweetfort at all?* she wondered. *What if Klaus decided to wait back at home for Molasses to return with confirmation of a plot?* She thought on that while she studied her surroundings for signs of her friends. Knowing Klaus's character, she gathered that he would not back down from a fair challenge, and she understood that he needed to solidify himself as a worthy king in the eyes of both his dubious followers and the Voles of Cowtown. *No, he left Sweetfort with three-fourths of the Alliance according to Molasses's suggestion, I'm sure of it. But where is he? It wouldn't be easy to miss a hundred mice and cookies marching their way through the grass.*

They went on for another minute or two without seeing anything of note, but then Ginger thought she saw movement ahead in not one area, but in three; she strained her eyes to get a better look, but whatever objects were moving seemed to be spooked by Trot and quickly hid behind the nearest tufts of grass. Molasses, lowering his looking glass from one eye, exchanged a glance with her to communicate that he had seen the same thing, but that he was unsure of what it had been.

"Those were our quarries!" said Agapa, still swinging from the fishing line in the back. "Klaus's strategy was sound. Instead of arranging the entirety of the Fur-Crumb Alliance in a single procession, he divided them in three. If one group was attacked, the others could come in from other angles and surround the ambushers."

"That sounds like Klaus!" Reinhard chimed in.

"The three groups saw us and retreated into the brush," Dave pointed out. "How are we going to convince them that it's us?"

"Trot, slow down, please," said Molasses. "Get a little bit closer to the groups and come to a complete stop. I have an idea."

"Whatever you say, little buddy," the bird replied, and he did as Molasses asked.

Once they had stopped, they paused for a moment to see if the mice would reveal themselves. When they failed to make an appearance, Molasses clambered up Trot's side and stood near his neck. Then he took his whisk from his back and lifted it high into the air with both arms.

"Klaus the mouse!" he called out in a booming voice. "King of Sweetfort, leader of the Colony Behind the Cabinets! Your friends are here! Come out, all of you! You're safe!"

They waited another several seconds, but nothing stirred except for the blades of grass driven by the wind.

Then Ginger thought she heard some heightened whispering, followed by a decisive, "I will go, my king." It was then that Chester the butler crept out from behind the tuft of grass and headed toward them, rubbing his paws together with obvious anxiety. But once he had seen that those before him (other than the turkey, of course) were familiar, his eyes brightened and he breathed out a loud sigh. His back straightened and his arms fell to his sides.

"Friends of King Klaus!" he cheered. "Ginger and Molasses and Horace and Agapa and Dave and Reinhard! It is so great to see you! How glad I am that you are not foes here to kill us!" He cleared his throat and, remembering himself, adopted his usual stiff and wooden demeanor. "I ventured out here of my own volition, having failed my dear king so very miserably this morning. Volsaph, that brute! How I loathe him." The muscles around his mouth twitched with the mere use of the vole's name. "I figured that if anyone were seeking to avail of guerilla tactics and lay upon us from the east, I, not my king, should fall first to their blade."

"You've done plenty, Chester," Klaus said, sounding exasperated as he popped out into open view. He was garbed in the armor that had been displayed in his house; the helmet encased his head but left his face revealed, his ears popped up between holes at the crest of the helmet, and the rest of his body appeared to be well-protected by the gold, spraypainted aluminum. "Despite my protestations, you've done more than enough. Not every foreign sound is an enemy, you know."

Ginger and Molasses hopped down from Trot and sprinted over to their friend. They each hugged him while the members of the Fur-Crumb Alliance, having realized that there was no danger, walked into open view and began to dot the landscape. Agapa, Dave, Reinhard, and Horace joined the assembly, and Ingrid gave Horace a mighty hug the moment she saw him.

"Thank Mr. Theo that we found you!" said Ginger. "Another thirty minutes or so, and it would have been too late."

"Too late?" Klaus looked back and forth between her and Molasses. "Too late for what? What did you find out?"

"Volsaph's duel is nothing more than a charade," Molasses explained. "He just wanted you and the Alliance exposed and vulnerable."

"Vulnerable to what? Were they planning to attack?"

"They weren't planning to lift a single claw," Ginger told him. Then she spent the next few minutes filling Klaus in on every detail, from Tanas's new property and succulent produce, to his pact with the voles, to their conspiracy to use turkeys to extinguish the lives of their enemies. Although she had never really prided herself on her ability to tell a good story, she received many promising reactions from the crowd, and she was quite sure one elderly mouse matron nearly fainted at hearing the news. The cookies, on the other hand—Butter, Cinna, Mon, Van, Illa, Snowbank—seemed more furious than alarmed. Ginger understood their sentiments well. Their dangerous adversary was still employing his ungodly machinations in his attempt to get back at his father and ruin the old baker's creatures, and he had been all too close at succeeding.

Klaus crossed his arms, his aluminum armor crinkling with the movement. "The devil! The voles have always been morally compromised, and Tanas capitalized on that weakness. Their alliance, deplorable as it is, makes sense; they both have ambitions for the vale, although their goals are different. King Chisha wants the land of Sprinklevale...."

"And Tanas wants the hearts," Molasses finished for him.

"That's right. But mark my words: neither of them will get what they want." He placed a paw in the spot where Molasses's shoulder might have been. "It was good of you to act on your instincts. You knew Volsaph was hiding something, and because you followed up on that feeling, you've managed to save many lives. Cookies and mice alike, myself included, are in your debt—and in the debt of those who were by your side in this journey." He then walked past his friends and bowed before the turkey who had, surprisingly, remained quiet during the entire exchange. "Trot, is it? My name is Klaus. I must also thank you for ferrying my friends over here in such a timely manner. It sounds like they couldn't have done it without you." He extended his arm to the bird. "Now put 'er there!"

Trot's eyes grew large, and he reached out a single wing in disbelief and brushed it against Klaus's paw. "I love this mouse already. He knows the ways of my flock, and he looks like some sort of legendary hero of legend! Look at that sword! It's bigger than his body!"

Ginger, hesitant to interrupt, waved one of her arms. "I don't disagree that everyone here is heroic, but the day isn't over yet. The turkeys have probably left the forest already, and if so, they will reach Great Boris's Stump any minute now. They're running faster than any mouse I've ever seen. Klaus, you need to have the Fur-Crumb Alliance retreat and hide before the turkeys swarm the field. The only way to outpace them is to flee *right now*."

"Then that's what we'll do," answered Klaus. "The woods of Mount Oniz are not far from here. I think we'll be safe there."

"Um...Klaus, a word, if I may?" asked Molasses. "Privately? You, Ginger, and myself?"

"Of course."

They moved to the side, and Ginger watched as Trot moseyed over to the members of the Alliance. The bird began to speak with Ingrid and a few others, his voice heightened with excitement. Some of the cookies approached him, having never seen a turkey up close before. Half of the mice kept their distance, likely unable to view a turkey as anything other than a predator.

"There's one last thing we need to share with you, Klaus," said Molasses.

Klaus pointed to the top of his helmet. "I'm all ears."

"Bahar told us that half the vole kingdom is bivouacked in the northwestern part of Lakeview Thicket. They intended to watch the massacre and celebrate their victory from that location."

"That doesn't surprise me. They're cowards through and through."

"Maybe it's time that we got back at those cowards?"

Ginger narrowed her eyes. "For revenge, Brother?"

He turned his head to her, and she was pleased to see that his eyes betrayed not a hint of bloodthirst. "For justice. Doesn't one of Mr. Theo's own letters say that he who digs a pit will fall into it, and that a stone will roll back upon the one who rolls it?"

"Yes," said Ginger. "Mr. Theo has also told us that we reap what we have sown."

"Then the voles will reap what they have sown," Klaus replied, nodding. "They sowed malice and will harvest judgment. Their wickedness will come back on their own heads."

"Exactly what I was thinking," said Molasses. "But how are we going to get that done?"

Klaus looked at Ginger, a gleam in his eye. "I believe we'll need the help of our dear negotiator."

CHAPTER 7
Harvest

I can't believe we're doing this, thought Ginger as she gazed out at Great Boris's Stump, which was growing nearer every second. *We're going to be eaten alive. These turkeys won't care if we taste like rosemary. I could be dipped in marmalade, and they would* still *eat me. I'm sure of it.*

She, Klaus, and Molasses were standing on Trot's back, clinging to his feathers and hurrying toward the western end of the turkey run. They were about a mile from their target, as far as she could tell, but even from here she could see that the crazed birds were on the verge of finishing their race and scattering across the field. By now it was well into the afternoon, maybe an hour from the time that Volsaph had originally set for the "duel," and the clouds pinkened with the light of sunset. Night seemed to fall quickly at this time of the year, and the idea of running around in the field in the dark was one that worried Ginger. If they were providentially able to complete their mission, there was still the long journey home in a field that teemed with coyotes, opossums, and other critters. Even the lower slopes of Mount Oniz were not exempt from the occasional intruders that sought prey away from their usual haunts.

"You both did well," Klaus told them, the fur of his face undulating with the wind. "If there were any doubts from the mice who defected from King Shol as to the integrity and trustworthiness of the Cookies of Theo, you've laid those doubts to rest. You've only further strengthened the bonds of the Alliance."

"We weren't doing it for any kind of reward or notoriety," answered Molasses, "nor to prove ourselves to anyone. But if that's the happy byproduct...well, I'm not complaining."

Ginger tried to ignore the thought that the three leaders of the Alliance were charging into probable peril.

"Your mice mean as much to us as they do to you, Klaus. We may be two species, but we're of one mind, one purpose, one fate. Not to mention, this time our enemies intended to hurt both mice *and* cookies. That means Tanas sees the Alliance as a threat."

"Or an annoyance," Molasses offered.

"Maybe both," said Klaus. "Either way, it's a good thing. I can only hope that, with time, our enemies learn to fear us so deeply that they dare not attack."

"Don't give them too much credit," Ginger told him. "They seem a little slow on the uptake."

"You're saying they're stupid?"

"In some ways, yes."

After they had passed the stump, it was a short dash before they reached the spot where the two high walls of the turkey run ended. Ginger pulled Molasses's looking glass from his belt and put it to her eye to get a good look at the approaching stampede. The group of birds was led by two hens who appeared, paradoxically, both big-bodied and gaunt. A wildness filled their eyes and the eyes of all those behind them, and they glanced every which way; Ginger knew that the thought of their rumbling bellies and weak legs was all that filled their minds, and she wondered if the poor dears would last another day without their appetites sated. Their gobbles were loud and forceful, almost as though they were threatening anyone who stood between them and their destination. Trot stopped right at the end of the turkey run, and Ginger felt her confidence draining with every step of the nearing crowd.

"Move it, Trot!" demanded the hen on Ginger's right. "Tanas promised us a smorgasbord in northern Sprinklevale. We need to eat, or we'll die."

"I understand that!" Trot shouted back. "But hear us out! Please, we just need your attention for a minute. Maybe less. Depends how fast my friend here talks."

The hens groaned and slowed until they had stopped about a human arm's length from Trot, the others braking behind them. Upon a quick count, Ginger tallied thirty to forty birds, more than enough to have made quick work of the Alliance. She stepped toward the back of Trot's body; an arm's length from the crazed fowl was too close for comfort. Molasses dropped back, as well, but Klaus stood his ground and drew his sword—whether as a warning or as a frightened response, she could not guess. She could even feel Trot's body shaking beneath her, a sensation that did not, in any way, fill her with courage.

"What in Fair Felicia's Flattering Feathers do you want now?" asked the hen on Ginger's left. "Do you want to tell us you were right? Or do you have more conspiracy theories to share with us?"

"I'd rather hear about why he has walking food riding on his back," said the first turkey, licking her beak.

"Firstly, yes, I was totally right about my Tanas theory, as your empty stomachs can attest," said Trot. "Well, mostly right. I didn't have *all* the details, but I knew he was up to no good! Secondly, no, I'm fresh out of conspiracy theories for the day, but check back with me tomorrow. And these are my friends, not your appetizers. Pretty sure gingerbread is bad for our digestive tracts, anyway."

"So why have you stopped us, then?" asked the hen on the right, her tone betraying her impatience.

Trot threw a glance toward his back. "They're ready. It's all you, Ms. Cookie."

Ginger, her legs shaking harder than Trot's body, inched forward with reluctance. When she had reached the front of his body, she touched his neck. "May I?"

"Certainly."

Klaus and Molasses gave her a boost, and with much grunting, she managed to shimmy up the turkey's curved neck. When she had reached the top of her friend's head, he stood up straight so that she was able to look out at the entire flock. Something flipped inside where her stomach would have been; she had never really liked heights all that much, and seeing three dozen predators staring at her did not make it any better. *I'm going to pass out*, she thought. *Yep, any moment now. Either that or throw up. Am I capable of throwing up? What would even come out? Good golly, Ginger, stop thinking about throwing up*!

"I love her bow!" remarked a random turkey in the group after a prolonged silence.

"Right?" said Trot. "That's what I said. It's a marvelous piece of fashion."

Ginger held her arms out as a way of maintaining her balance. "Hello, everyone! My name is Ginger, and I want to say that I'm glad to have your attention at this critical hour. I know you're starving, so I'll get to the point.

"As you remember, Tanas promised you protection from the hunters in this region and had King Chisha's mice convince you to fill his barn. Sure, he kept his promise; you're alive, right? You weren't hunted. But at what cost? All these months he has withheld food from you. Did you ask yourselves why? Was it cruelty, or was he planning to use your hunger for something sinister? A mix of both, I'm afraid."

"But he promised a feast this evening," said the hen on the right, sounding less sure of herself.

"And maybe he would have kept that promise, too," responded Ginger. "But that was after you starved for a month. Let me tell you a secret, all of you. Tanas hates me, and he hates my brother here. He hates all of us cookies who remain loyal to the one who made us—Mr. Theo, who lives in the house overlooking Sprinklevale. Not long after I came to life at Mr. Theo's hand, Tanas, his son, was there, offering me promises. Like you, I thought he had my best interest at heart. What I later realized was that his promises were backed by a motive to bring harm to others, and so I spurned his offer, and he has despised me and those like me ever since.

"We Cookies of Theo had a series of adventures with King Klaus of the Mice of Sweetfort here, along with his kin. Eventually, we formed an alliance and agreed that we would fight our battles together. Our fates are now intertwined with those of Klaus and his fellow mice. Tanas knows this, and he hates these mice, maybe as much as he hates us cookies. That's why he hatched a plan to have the Alliance come to the stump behind me under a false pretense; his goal was to have you, overcome with hunger, consume every last one of us. You would have done so without a second thought, and because Tanas would have kept his promise, perhaps he would have even gained your respect. Who knows what other plans he could have concocted, using you to do his bidding?"

"He—he didn't really care about keeping us safe?" one of the turkeys asked. "He didn't care about sparing us?"

"Only insofar as it served his agenda. If he didn't have you around, he couldn't launch his plan to kill us. So he kept you alive—but just barely, it seems."

"Do you really think that's why he let us go hungry?" a turkey asked his neighbor.

"It makes sense," replied the other. "The cookie is right. I was ready to feast on anything that I saw. I wouldn't have thought twice about it."

"Tanas thought he could control us?" inquired a third. "What a tool!"

The hen on the left took a step forward. "What respect *I* had for Tanas was lost when he forced us to go hungry. We protested, but he wouldn't hear it. That respect can't be won back. Even if he had kept his promise and we were now feasting on your...alliance, that would've been it. We would've never worked with the man again." She shook her head, her wattle jiggling. "That said, we're still famished. Regardless of what Tanas did or didn't do, we need to eat. If your friends are out there, we won't eat them out of obedience to Tanas, but because we're too hungry not to."

"Aren't you listening to Ms. Cookie?" grumbled Trot. "She and her alliance don't deserve this!"

"You're a turkey, Trot. You know very well that we eat not because our prey deserves it, but because of our instinct, our *need*. It's no different this time."

"What if I had a counterproposal?" Ginger asked her. "What if there was a way for you to satisfy your hunger and get retribution for the suffering that Tanas put you through?"

The bird cocked her head to the side and glanced at those around her. "Well, now that's an interesting thought. What do you propose?"

Ginger gestured toward the northeast, where Lakeview Thicket cupped the land and ended at the base of Mount Oniz. "King Chisha knew of Tanas's deceit and did nothing to help you. He was complicit in coaxing you into the barn, as were all those voles who convinced you that you would be safe and well-cared-for on his property. Half of their forces wait in that section of the forest over there, hoping to witness a great victory over their enemies. Their goal is to take Sprinklevale from the Mice of Sweetfort, and they sided with Tanas to achieve that goal. If you go after them, you will get back at both Chisha and Tanas, and you will spare those who have done nothing to harm you."

The hen on the right narrowed her eyes. "How do we know you're not trying to pull something like Tanas? How can we trust you?"

"Because whether you go after King Chisha's voles or not, as long as you spare the ones we love, you can consider us friends. We expect nothing of you and make no promises other than friendship. And you can see that we hate Tanas and his schemes; hopefully you feel the same way about him, and if you do, then we have a common enemy."

The two turkeys who had led the march to Sprinklevale looked at Ginger for some time, unspeaking, as if they were trying to discern whether there was deceit in her words. At length, they turned to each other and talked in hushed voices that were punctuated by a nod here or a shaking of the head there. Then they included several other turkeys in their discussion, and now their voices were climbing with either excitement or distress, their wings flapping to emphasize the points they made. Finally, the hen on the left turned back to Ginger, tilted her head, and unleashed a series of three gobbles.

"Is that a good thing?" Klaus asked Trot.

"I have no idea," confessed the bird. "They don't share a single code with me nowadays. Something about me being a 'blabbermouth,' whatever that means."

"We'll spare your alliance and head to the northwestern part of the forest on one condition," said the hen. "If you're unwilling, then each turkey will go where he or she pleases and feast as he or she pleases."

"Fine," replied Ginger. "What are your terms?"

"You seem earnest enough, but after all we've been through, we fear another trap. For that reason, we ask that you lead the charge atop Trot. Bring us to the forest and prove there's no danger for us; then you can go your way, and we'll go ours."

Molasses nudged Klaus. "That could be dangerous. The voles might see us coming and lay an ambush for us."

But Ginger and Klaus shared a knowing look and nodded at each other. *Trot is fast enough*, he was telling her with his eyes. *We'll get away in time. It's worth the risk.* She turned her attention to the turkeys once more. "We're agreed; we'll lead the way and prove that it's safe."

"That's what I like to hear!" Trot declared, his feathers bristling. "Now come on, family! Let's show those voles not to mess with the Fur-Crumb Alliance *or* us turkeys. To the forest!"

The Voles of Cowtown did not know what hit them. Although some of the ranks on the edge of the forest spotted the incoming birds and attempted to flee, they were nowhere near as fast as their attackers, and the turkeys had breached the forest before the retreating voles had gone more than a few feet. After Trot had made it beneath the canopy of leaves, he turned to the north and allowed his kin to sweep through the lines of their foes. Ginger placed her arms over her eyes to avoid watching the onslaught, but because she still had a hole in her left arm, she was forced to watch. She quickly lost count of how many voles were consumed by the ravenous birds, but she guessed that there were perhaps fifty in a few minutes' time. Although some turned to fight with their toothpick swords or twig bows, it was a hopeless endeavor; the weapons bounced off the turkeys' feathers the way a smooth stone bounces off the surface of water, leaving their targets unharmed.

A few of the voles managed to creep away in the chaos, and Molasses pointed out Volsaph, who was heading northeast into an area that had not yet been touched by the turkeys. When Molasses mentioned that this was the vole who had challenged Klaus to a duel that was never to take place, Trot flew into a rage and burst between the trees after the creature. Ginger noticed that Klaus drew his sword again as they made their approach, but he did not get a chance to slay his deceiver; Trot, flapping his wings like a beast gone mad, lowered his head, opened his beak, and scooped up Volsaph in a single lunge. Klaus blinked with surprise and returned his sword to its position. *I suppose it's fair*, thought Ginger. *Volsaph never intended to fight Klaus in hand-to-hand combat, anyway. He chose the coward's path and died a coward's death. Although I sure would have liked to see Klaus wipe the forest floor with him.*

The turkeys spread out in every direction, snatching up the few voles who had managed to escape the initial assault. They did not stop to thank her and her friends for the meal to which she had directed them, nor did they seem all that interested in formalizing a treaty or alliance—not at that moment, at least. As they finished their feast, they continued deeper into the forest with many satisfied and cheery gobbles along the way. And then they were gone, the marks of their talons and a few stray scraps of vole clothing the only signs that they had ever been there.

"Each of them will find a tree to perch in, where they'll sleep for the night," said Trot. "This will be the first content sleep they will have had in over a month, thanks to you. Their contentment isn't just because of their full bellies, but because you gave them an alternative to the evil plot of Tanas, his name be cursed forever! I'm glad they made the right choice."

"Believe me," Klaus replied, "so are we."

"And now you all can enjoy a nice Harvest supper together." The bird's eyes moved here and there as he stopped to think. "Oh, but wait! You're far from home, aren't you? And the sun is saying, 'Adieu' for the night. That's...too bad."

Molasses sighed and held his arms out helplessly. "There's not really anything we can do about that, unfortunately."

"Nonsense! I could ferry you back home before the sun goes all the way down! Yeah, I'm sure of it! All...ninety-six members of your alliance."

Klaus laughed. "You're fast, Trot, but I don't even think one of those vehicles on wheels could make it to town *that* fast. And there's not enough room for the entire Alliance."

"Aw, well...." Trot nodded in understanding. "Yeah, maybe you're right. But I do think we're a pretty good team, all of us. If ever you need to get somewhere quickly in the future, I'm your guy."

"I have a feeling we'll be taking you up on that sooner than you can guess, Trot. And I thank you for the kind offer."

Ginger frowned at her murine friend. "I'm sorry that you did all that setting up in your house this morning for no purpose. We would have been preparing to sit down for Harvest dinner right now. Instead, we're here...in this dark forest, away from home and comfort."

"That may be," Klaus said with a shrug, "but at least we're together. The Fur-Crumb Alliance is just around the corner. And as for Harvest dinner...well, we're all here, and there are plenty of nuts in this forest."

"Nuts?" asked Trot. "My friends aren't nuts. We're all perfectly sane."

"No, *nuts*. Acorns, walnuts...."

"Oh, got it."

Klaus smiled. "I'm sure we'll have a feast of our own in a matter of minutes. And I think I have just the place for our Harvest dinner."

They did not have to travel far before they reached the northeastern corner of the forest, which ended where a great lake, known as Lake Sysba, which possessed the shape of a left-tilting crescent moon, began. The gentle waves lapped against the dirt and against the bark of a few trees, and the placid central portion of the lake reflected the blushing clouds. Just as Ginger and her friends reached a flat and leafless area overlooking the lake, the rest of the Fur-Crumb Alliance drew near from the west, many of them bearing the varieties of nuts that Klaus had mentioned. Ingrid led the group, trailed closely by Horace, Agapa, Dave, and Reinhard. Smiles extended across their faces, smiles that told Ginger they knew that their foes were fallen and that they had expected to feast in the forest this evening. Even Ingrid herself was lugging an acorn that looked far too big for her to carry, judging by the way she swayed under its weight. Klaus noticed, hurried over to her, and took on the burden himself. He then directed the Alliance to the flat area and dropped the acorn, an act that the others mirrored.

There were no banners, shining lights, wreaths, or even tables or plates; however, Ginger's first Harvest dinner felt no less than perfect. The members of the Alliance broke off into small groups and used rocks as their seats, forming circles across the open land. Ginger was pleased to see that her fellow cookies had befriended the mice and, instead of sitting off to the side with their own kind, voluntarily scattered themselves among their rodent allies. A few mice used the cupules of acorns to scoop fresh water from the lake and passed them around. The cookies had no need for food or drink but shared a thankful smile and handed the provisions over to the nearest mouse. Within the hour night had fallen completely, and autumn's chill settled on the forest. Seeing that the mice were shivering, Molasses disappeared up the slope of Mount Oniz for several minutes and returned holding miniature torches. Ginger assumed he had gone to the nearest road entrance to Mount Oniz, for every afternoon, when Mr. Theo came home from town, he set large torches aflame on either side of the main roads at the base of his mountain. These lights in the darkness were meant to serve as guides for those who desired to fellowship with the man; thus, Ginger thought it was fitting that Molasses had taken parts of these torches to provide light and warmth for the allies of those whom Mr. Theo loved.

Her group was the one nearest the lake and was comprised of herself, Klaus, Ingrid, Molasses, Agapa, Dave,

Reinhard, Horace, and Trot. It was the nine of them for the first couple of hours, but then a figure approached from outside the light that was cast by the torch standing in the center of their circle. Klaus and Molasses both reached for their weapons and stood side by side to bar the possible foe's access to their friends. But once Molasses saw that it was Bahar, his body eased; in response, Klaus took a step back and extended a paw to signal that Molasses should speak with the rodent.

"Would you kind mice and cookies be willing to accept the company of a poor, lone vole like myself?" the creature asked, tapping his claws together and avoiding eye contact. "It seems that I'm no longer welcomed in Cowtown."

"Bahar," said Molasses, beaming and patting his friend's arm.

"The one who was willing to betray his own kinsmen for the sake of doing what was right," Klaus said, taking Bahar's paw in his own. "I'm quite familiar with that sentiment, you know. If you are willing to be despised and even hunted for doing good, then yes, you have a place here. You'll find that most of us here feel the same as you." He released the vole's paw and stood up straight. "King Klaus of the Mice of Sweetfort."

"Bahar."

Klaus clapped his paws together. "Bahar, welcome! You've come at the right time. We were just about to share what we're thankful for. Newbies get to go first. King's rules, you know."

The group laughed, and one by one, they began to express their gratitude. Bahar and Trot were thankful for new friends and for no unplanned alien abductions that year (respectively); Horace was relieved that he had had "one more adventure" in him, that his hips had held up better than expected, and that he had finally met a vole that he liked; Reinhard was glad that his clumsiness in the attic had not resulted in the untimely demise of their party, and that he had much of Mr. Theo's letters memorized so he could recite the man's words to himself throughout the day; Dave was thankful to have ventured into Cowtown and lived to tell the tale, and for befriending a turkey; Agapa was grateful for Mr. Theo's love, which was the most powerful love that a cookie could know, and for her opportunity to enable other cookies to fall in love and grant them a small peek into the magnitude of their creator's love for them; Ingrid was glad that her husband had been spared what could have been an ugly duel (had Volsaph not been lying, of course), and that the Alliance had been spared a painful fate at the beaks of the turkeys. After Ingrid finished speaking, Klaus nodded at Molasses, and the cookie stood in the center of the circle, beside the flickering torch.

"You know," he said, "it's easy to mourn what could have been. We could sit around and bemoan the fact that we aren't sitting in Klaus's cozy home right now, enjoying Sweetfort in all its glory. But when we think of what could have been, we often forget what *was*. Almost five months ago, my sister and Klaus were lost to us. They were wasting away in King Shol's prison, but to us they were as good as dead, and we almost gave up hope of ever seeing them again. But now they're here, and they're safe. We're all safe, and we're together. I also--" He looked at the ground before meeting Ginger's gaze. "Going back farther, I was a rogue cookie, following Tanas's whims...."

"Curséd be his name!" Trot cried out, scaring everyone in the vicinity.

"...and separated from my sister," Molasses continued. "But we have been working side by side all day, for the good of others. I was not her enemy. I was not scouring the vale for her. She was with me, and we faced the day together. I could not be more thankful."

Klaus rose from his rock with a grunt. "I never knew you could be so sappy, Molasses. No pun intended." He looked at those sitting around him as Molasses returned to his seat. "Well, my friends, what can I say? One year ago, I was on the run from King Shol, hiding in a nook behind a cabinet, not knowing where the rebellion of myself and my fellow mice would lead. There was so much uncertainty, and fear, and struggle. But then a certain cookie came along—"

"Ms. Cookie!" shouted Trot, smacking Ginger in the side with a feather. "He's talking about you!"

"Yes, Ginger, also known as 'Ms. Cookie.'"

"She'll be 'Mrs. Cookie' some day soon!" the turkey predicted. "Mark my words!"

Klaus chuckled. "I guess we'll find out, won't we? But she came along, and through her friendship and the guidance of Mr. Theo, this alliance was formed. And who am I, that I should be among such amazing, honorable mice and cookies? If I could only break this crown into pieces and have each of you wear it. I'm no more worthy than any one of you."

Ingrid fleeced her whiskers in obvious anxiety. "It's just a figure of speech, everyone. My dear, lovely husband wouldn't break his beautiful crown into pieces, would he?"

"I suppose I just want to say that...Ginger, I'm thankful for our friendship, which has extended into unforeseen spheres and helped so many. Friends, I am thankful for our alliance, for it is by the work of this alliance that lives were saved today. And Ingrid, I'm thankful for having your tiny paw in marriage, because there is no one in all the world who is lovelier or better suited to this humbled, undeserving mouse."

He sat down once more and beckoned Ginger to stand. She walked over to the torch and placed her right arm against it. "Saving the best for last, Klaus?" she teased. "What am I thankful for? How can I narrow it down to just a few things? This morning, Reinhard quoted our maker, who told us to be thankful in all circumstances. I have been asking myself if that is true of me. Am I thankful in all circumstances? My brother, who is in many ways more mature than I am, said we sometimes mourn what could have been. I'm guilty of that, friends. I wanted the extravagant celebration in Klaus's house. I wanted uninterrupted time with all of you. I wanted to have a normal holiday for once. But I didn't get that. Instead, Tanas had to be...well, Tanas, and throw a wrench into our plans." She sighed. "I've been struggling with mourning what could have been ever since Independence Day, when I was locked in prison. But I realized something today. If I hadn't been locked in prison,

Molasses wouldn't have sought me. If he hadn't sought me, he wouldn't have met Bahar. If he hadn't met Bahar, then we probably would have died in that attic today. If we had died in that attic today, then nothing would have stopped the turkeys from swarming the fields and eating every mouse and cookie they came across.

"When we mourn what could have been, it's easy to be bitter rather than thankful. But if we had gotten what *could* have been rather than what came to be, we wouldn't have what we have. An alliance. New friends. Each other. We wouldn't have any of it." She thought of the lamb cookie and what he had relayed to her in Tanas's garden. "I'm still learning, but thankfully, I have a maker who is so very patient with me, who forgives me, and who ensures there is nothing that comes into my life that can't be used for my good and for his renown. I'm thankful for the best brother in the world, Molasses. For the best friend and mouse in the world, Klaus. And I'm thankful for all of you—for your comradery, and for fighting for what is good. Final victory is near. I truly believe that."

A few among the group clapped and cheered, and very shortly thereafter they returned to their individual conversations. Some of them, including Reinhard and Trot, led the Alliance in a dancing song, and many cookies and mice began to shake and wiggle and jig. Klaus looked at Ginger and patted the stone beside him, indicating that she should sit. She considered it for a second, but instead she turned around and walked across the flat ground, over the moist fallen leaves, and to the edge of the lake. There she could see that the clouds had broken in a few areas and that there was only a sliver of moon to be seen in the sky, its gold surface reflected by the still water. She found a small mound of grass on which she sat to gaze at the breathtaking vista.

Klaus came to her side a minute later and sat on the ground, his tail forming a thin trail in the dirt behind him. Although there had been no need for his armor, he had not taken it off, and it gleamed prettily in the moonlight. He looked not at her but at the lake, following her gaze. "By my whiskers, Ginger! It's not like you to be aloof while others are celebrating a holiday. I mean, you *are* the most festive cookie in the world, after all."

"That hasn't changed, Klaus, trust me," she replied with a small smile, tapping one of her cornucopia buttons with the end of her left arm.

"I know it hasn't. And come this time next month, you'll be staring at Christmas ornaments like a fat child stares at cake. Is that the expression humans use?"

"Close enough, I think. You got your point across, at least."

He touched a tendril of grass that sprouted from the ground next to him. "So what bothers you this pleasant, victorious night?"

She shifted in the grass until she faced him. "I saw Tanas earlier today, Klaus. He was standing in the window of his house just north of Cowtown. That's the first time I've seen him since the night before Christmas last year."

"And do you think he saw you, too?"

"I'm not sure. Maybe. But it just—it solidified in my mind that he isn't far away. He's *right there*, and he's still up to his antics. What he tried to do with the turkeys was so barbaric, so brazen. I can't help but wonder what else he has up his sleeve. I mean, Molasses said we're safe, but for how long? You say that lives were saved today, but for how much longer will they be spared? I think Tanas is planning something else. I learned today that I can't stand against him in my own strength; it's futile."

"What do you mean, you learned you can't stand against him?"

"Oh! Um...nothing, really." She had said too much, but she could not back out now. "Molasses and I kind of...charged toward his house."

"You did *what*? You *charged toward his house*?" Klaus looked hurt. "And without me?"

Surprised by that, she let out a giggle. "You're the best and strongest mouse I know, but even you—maybe even the entire Alliance—wouldn't be able to stand against Tanas. It's not just his influence on a grand scale that is scary, Klaus. He has influence on an *individual* scale, and I'm ashamed to say that both Molasses and I were seconds away from giving in to his targeted temptation. Just like we were at the beginning." She looked down at the grass rising up from beneath her. "We are still so weak, and he is so strong. But don't worry! By the power that our maker supplied, Molasses and I snapped out of our daze and decided not to throw our lives away in some sort of foolhardy assault."

"Well, that's good. You would have given this old mouse a broken heart."

"You're not *that* old, Klaus." She put the end of her arm to where her chin might have been. "Just kind of old. For a mouse."

He chuckled. "Well, as far as Tanas goes, haven't you told me that Mr. Theo promised to take care of him?"

"Ultimately, yes. But in the meantime...we can only guess what havoc he plans to wreak on us, on Sprinkleton, and on surrounding regions."

Klaus seemed to mull that over for a moment. Then he rose from the earth and reached a paw out to her. "Let's trust that he'll reap a harvest of judgment of his own. But that's another battle for another day, my dear Ginger—and one for which we will prepare. I promise. Now let's not worry about tomorrow; there are enough worries for the day. Shall we return to our celebration?"

She smiled at him. "We shall," she answered.

He pulled her up from the grass, and she proceeded to follow him toward their circle of friends where Trot was singing, loudly and very much out of tune, while the cookies and mice danced around him. Before she could reenter the flat area beneath the trees, she thought she heard something moving behind her. It was an unwelcome sound, a stinging sound, a *hungry* sound—and it seemed to be coming from the water. She turned back around and sauntered toward the lake to see if she could get a better look at whatever had broken the silence of the night, but there was nothing more than a few ripples that became waves. Then something emerged from the water, something that felt dark and ancient. For a moment she saw her own reflection in the creature's scales before it slipped back beneath the waves of the lake.

THE
END

Made in the USA
Las Vegas, NV
26 November 2024